Goodnight Drinks

Goodnight Drinks

Gary Smillie

Matador
Unit E2 Airfield Business Park,
Harrison Road, Market Harborough,
Leicestershire. LE16 7UL
Tel: 0116 2792299
Email: books@troubador.co.uk
Web: www.troubador.co.uk/matador
Twitter: @matadorbooks

ISBN 978 1803132 822
British Library Cataloguing in Publication Data.
A catalogue record for this book is available from the British Library.

Typeset in 11pt Minion pro by Troubador Publishing Ltd, Leicester, UK

Matador is an imprint of Troubador Publishing Ltd

For Wendy Louise and Gary William Smillie,
my wonderful mum and dad.

Contents

The Wrong Side
of the Mirror

She had been noticing how everything meant the opposite. Politicians. The manufacturers of cars and their advertising lackeys. Broadcast corporations who claimed they cared about racism. When they said, or wrote or broadcast something, anything actually, what they really meant was the complete opposite of whatever they had said or written or broadcast.

We are serious about tackling poverty. Leading the fight for a greener planet. Black lives matter. Then a friend of hers said this, in a conversation:

"I know, mate. Black is white and white is black. We're through the fucking looking glass." (Mate)

And that might have been what planted the seed. Anyway, it all happened pretty soon after that.

It was about three or four nights later. She was brushing her teeth in the en-suite bathroom. Behind her, a band of yellow light from the open door was cast across the big, moustached face of her snoring husband. He always got to sleep before her. It was like he didn't have anything to think about. There was so much to think about in the world, so much that needed fixing, but it didn't seem to matter to him. He went down and he was out. It had been like that all thirty years of their marriage and she envied him for it. Even hated him for it, a bit. She, on the other hand, could never switch the thoughts off. And there were more and more of them, multiplying, the older she got.

She turned to look at her own face in the mirror. She started the familiar exercise of counting the lines and categorising them: new, newish, old, wretched, but she soon got sick of it. Instead, she started trying to look at the mirror itself. Perhaps you have tried to do this. It isn't easy, of course. How can you see the mirror itself, when all it shows you is a reflection? It hides behind that reflection, the mirror. The real mirror is not the crow's feet by your tired eyes, you need to ignore those; they are distractions. The real mirror is that little bit deeper. It is below the surface. She started to think about what her friend had said. Then she saw something move.

This movement was not on her side of the mirror, it was behind. The moment she saw it, she was sure of that. Something was moving inside the mirror. It looked like a waving hand, but it was gone as soon as it was glimpsed. Strange, she thought, then she thought of what to do next. She reached out and she tapped the mirror. The sound was hollow. What on earth? She thought. That can't be right. That should be all solid wall behind there. I mean, that's really strange. So she tapped again and the sound was deeper and longer. It was a real echo this time. Like banging on an empty metal silo with a clenched fist.

She looked behind her. Her husband was definitely sleeping. Dead as a rotting log, but for the guttural orchestra, as per usual. There was no way anything she did here would wake him. So she grabbed the mirror and pulled. Sure enough, it came away easy in her hands.

She put the glass down quietly on the ground, propping it against the toilet bowl. In the space behind the mirror there was a vast black emptiness so enormous and dense that it seemed to be generating its own magnetic force. She felt it pulling on her. It seemed to take her by the shoulders and hold her firmly. It seemed to look at her, this darkness, just as she looked at it. Clearly, it wanted very much to bring her inside. She stared into it a while, wondering if she would see the same movement again, the wave, but something told her she would not. The strangest thing of all was that she was not surprised by any of this. She was not afraid and she knew exactly what she should do. The only thing to do now was to go in.

She looked behind her quickly to check her husband was still sleeping. He was, so she grabbed the rim of the sink. She climbed up into the basin, unsure if it would take her weight, because her husband had fitted it himself to save on costs. It held firm. She crouched there and pushed her cheek to the black. It was cool and inviting. She glanced backward over her shoulder one last time, then she turned and climbed right in.

For a moment, she couldn't see anything. There was a blinding flash of brilliant white light, exactly like you expect when this magical kind of thing finally happens. She sightlessly found her footing on the reassuringly even ground of the other side and the air around her felt pleasantly mild. When the light flare passed, she found she was standing in an enormous public library, the kind they used to have, before rows and rows of beautifully bound books. She didn't need to read a sign to tell her where she was. She understood it. At once, she realised that she could trust things here, just as she saw them.

Before her, men, women and children strolled around the aisles of well stocked shelves, stopping to take down books and perusing them at their leisure. One man, standing at a large mahogany desk in the periodical section, looked up at her, smiled and waved. Could that have been the man she had seen, standing back in her en-suite bathroom, just moments ago? She didn't know, but she didn't much care either. She felt completely comfortable, there in the library and she reckoned there was time enough to work everything out, with so many seemingly pleasant, seemingly happy people milling about and so many books to consult.

Then, another thought. What about her husband? He was still back there, on the wrong side of the mirror, snoring his head off. She felt suddenly very guilty about the negative thoughts she'd had about his D.I.Y. capabilities and his wholly blameless ability to sleep well. She had to let him know where she was and what she'd been up to.

She turned around and saw his gurning face, suddenly enormous, right in front of her. It was a shock. Big, red and coarsely haired, his head was filling up more or less the whole space where the mirror had been. He looked baffled and was scratching his nose. Then he ducked out of view. Before she could act, before she guessed what was happening, his giant hands were looming over her, holding the glass pane of the mirror squarely and fixing it back into place.

She rushed towards him, but it was too late. She collided with the cool green rear of the reattached mirror. Vaguely, she could see his dark silhouette moving around on the other side, doing bathroomy things. She hit the glass, but he didn't seem to hear her. She could see his black marionette working a shadowy toothbrush up and down. She thumped the glass again. She started banging on the glass like a bloody mad woman. She wanted to tell him that things were better when you just stepped through. You just had to go past the screen and things made sense again. That side, the side they'd been living on, was the wrong one. But he just screwed up his face in their bathroom and examined an angry spot in the crease of his nostril. He couldn't see her. He couldn't understand her at all.

The Bee

When it got really warm, like actually hot, which was rare, like, but anyway, when it got like it was that day, then we always went to the bunker. The summer break of '95 was a really hot one and that day might have been the hottest of all of them. That isn't how or why I remember it, though.

There was nothing strange about the way the day started. We did the same as always, me and Finn. We'd filled his massive ex-army rucksack with stolen beers, cigarettes, crisps and sweets, the night before – then we'd met up early by *the meadows*. Our starting point was that little rickety stile there that marked the beginning of a line of fields not owned by farmers or private estates. They were kept aside by the council, or something. I'm not sure actually, but anyway, they ran, *the meadows*, straight out of the village in a lush green line for more than a mile before opening up into the wider countryside. Miles and miles of `luv-e-ley Welsh grass`, my old man used to say in a bad Welsh accent, annoyingly. We weren't from there, originally. We'd moved because of dad's work.

They had been put aside especially for us kids to play in, those meadows, or at least that's how it seemed to us. Even the adults seemed to know it – somewhere for us kids to sod off to

– get out of their hair. Them summers the meadows were always full of kids – our own massive playground – and hardly any adults to be seen, except your dog walkers or your occasional farmer that we riled enough to come and give us a chase. You couldn't have it nowadays, I suppose. Parents these days need to know where their kids are at all times; have devices to tell them just that, even, but back then it seemed like any kid our age or thereabouts spent the best part of every day there, in the meadows, building dens, climbing trees, stream jumping and hunting. But me and Finn were getting too old for that. We preferred to be alone. We just started out at the stile then made the long walk out to the bunker where we knew the littler kids, like my brother, wouldn't follow. He, Finn, usually brought his big brother's Gat gun too, if Declan wasn't already out somewhere, using it. I remember those times as happy. At least, compared to what came after.

That day Finn didn't have the Gat. I remember because I felt disappointed but, more than that, a bit suspicious of the flat way Finn shut down the question. No, he just said, with no explanation – as if it was a stupid thing to ask and there were other things more important to think on. The sun wasn't long up when we started walking, but the sweat had already started beading above Finn's dark, always furrowed brow and over his full lips. The tiny, crystal balls sat balancing between the sparse brown hairs of his moustache that was already coming through.

We were twelve years old. Finn, though it's not like I said this to his face, was a bit of a hero of mine. He was athletic and tall and always seemed to have tan from being outside. I was pale, a little bit chubby and suffered from asthma. We used to hang out in a bigger group before, but that year we'd started doing more stuff on our own. No outsiders, we said. We must have looked a strange pair, but that didn't seem to matter to Finn. He had chosen me over the other boys. He could have chosen any of them but he chose me. It made me like him even more.

Finn was even quieter than normal that morning, but I didn't mind. Our walk was only just starting so I felt fresh, no asthma yet, and it was nice to listen to the birds in the trees. A slight morning breeze occasionally slipped through the trees and got in under my T-shirt. Finn's too. It cooled you down. We were just strolling along and it felt like it was going to be a good day.

As we walked, Finn kept stooping to pick up stones and sticks from the worn path, then flinging them sluggishly into the deeper grass. It looked funny because of the heavy rucksack, every time he stooped and swung his arm he reminded me of a cartoon I'd seen of the Hunchback of Notre Dame or something. I told him that and he laughed and said, "The bells, the bells," but he soon went back to just throwing stuff in silence.

After about an hour's walking I suggested we stop and drink some water and eat some of the crisps. The sun was getting hotter and I was starting to wheeze a little and I hoped that he hadn't noticed. Finn agreed we should stop and sat down and took out the crisps and a big, green canteen that his dad had told him was exactly like the ones they used in the Falklands. We never drank the beer or smoked on the way to the bunker. We kept them for when we arrived.

We walked to the edge of the field and propped ourselves against the posts of a barbed wire fence. I ate all my crisps quickly, it was one of my skills, then did the thing with the packet when you make it into a kind of funnel and empty all the last bits into your mouth, like a mini dump truck at a fat human tip. Finn laughed a little when I said that, then tossed me the canteen casually. It was amazing, the easy way he did things. Everything all loose and effortless. Throwing things, especially, was his talent. He'd broke all the records for javelin at school. I noticed he wasn't really eating his crisps and felt somehow embarrassed about how quick I'd finished mine. He picked up a piece of grass and started chewing on it and looked into the distance. That was when he told me about the diary.

"So, can you keep a secret?" he asked.

I don't know why, but as soon as he asked that I felt so excited and nervous that I started to feel sick. Yes, I said, swallowing hard.

"I've taken my mum's diary," he said, "got it in the bag. I was looking for summat under their bed and it was under a floor board, so, you know… she defo doesn't want anyone to read it, nay."

Okay, I said, hiding my disappointment, and finding it strange that even though what he was saying should have been exciting, everything about the moment now felt somehow shitty.

"The thing is," he said, "I wasn't looking for it or nuffin, but you know, why was it under a floorboard? I mean, that's shady, nay?"

Finn had this North-Welsh dialect thing where he said *nay* at the end of almost every sentence. My dad hated it and would get angry when I used it at home, but I picked it up from Finn too and only lost it long after we moved away.

"And that's what made me think," Finn continued, "so I just took it, y' know. But I feel bad about it now, nay."

So, shall we read it then? I suggested, but he said no.

"Let's wait," he said. "We'll read it when we get there."

Then we just sat there for a bit, not saying anything. The sun was getting hot and the lush, damp grass steamed sweetly in the heat. Everything around us, the fences and the trees, the air even, seemed to hum. The smell, too, was heavy with something earthy, like the ground itself was ripe and ready to burst open or something. I remember it so clear. We were about to get up and go, when a bee flew out from the bushes behind the fence and started buzzing around Finn's head.

"Keep still," Finn said, in a strong, clear voice. He knew from before that I was scared of wasps and bees. I got stung one summer and my knee swelled up like a melon. I'd cried a lot, which was embarrassing, to be honest. Things like that, bee stings and anything dangerous, didn't seem to bother Finn, though.

I sat and watched as the bee buzzed loudly and hovered just inches from his face and he kept perfectly still. I think the bee could smell his sweat or something, because the sun was really getting up now and we both had a layer all over. I imagined if that was me, sitting there, how I'd feel. I'd have been up and running straight away. I'd have been flapping my arms everywhere, screaming. Finn didn't panic at all. He just stared at the bee as it dived toward, then away from his face, buzzing. Finn wasn't blinking. He even started to smile.

"Shhhhhhh, shhhhhhhhh, shhhhhhh," he said, the sound hushing out from his red lips like he was hypnotising the bee. It seemed to work. The bee got slower, its buzzing didn't sound so angry anymore, and before long it moved away from his face and settled on his shoulder.

I couldn't believe it. I always wished I could be like that, but it just didn't come natural. If I got scared by something, or excited, or whatever – it showed. But anyway, Finn, he just let the bee stay there. Let it walk around on him; crawling across his shoulder and his neck. Then he grinned at me. A big, proud grin.

"See," he said, "nuthin to worry about, nay." Then as soon as he'd said that the bee flew off, straight up into the blue sky.

"Goodbye Mr. Bee," said Finn, smiling up into the sun and blinking, finally.

***

Pretty soon we were up and walking again. I left it about ten minutes before mentioning the diary.

What do you think she writes in there? I said, dirty stuff? I blushed when I said it and felt bad, but Finn didn't really react.

"Dunno," he said, after a while, "Usual diary stuff, I suppose. Feelings, shit like that."

I asked Finn if he had ever kept a diary and he said he hadn't, but a little too quickly. What type of stuff would you write in one, I asked him, while looking in the other direction so that it seemed I wasn't really thinking about what I said that much.

"Survival stuff," said Finn, "Y'know – like an army one – exercises, rations, data about missions. That kind of shit, nay."

Finn was really into the army because his dad had been a sergeant when he was little. Finn said his dad had been in the Falklands, though I'd heard some of the other lads from the estate saying that wasn't true. They said that his dad wasn't even in the real army, but something called the TA. They never said it in front of Finn though, because he went schitz when people talked about his dad. Anyway, I didn't know either way and it didn't really bother me.

Apart from all the army stuff, Finn didn't really talk about his family and I didn't either. There wasn't much to say. Both our dads did normal jobs. Finn's dad worked at the mine, my dad worked in Chester and did something boring with computers, which he always said were 'the future', annoyingly, though it turns out he was right. Our mums both stayed at home, so there really wasn't much to say there either. That's why it was so strange that he had his Mum's diary that day. It felt like it was breaking our own rule; the *no outsiders* rule. It felt like there was someone else with us on the walk, but I didn't want to say anything in case it pissed him off.

When we arrived at the bunker it was past midday. The sun was high above us. Finn showed me this way of telling the time with a compass and a stick. He'd done it a few times before, but I checked on my watch to be sure without saying. It was proper baking by this point. We both had big patches on our T-shirts and sweat was dripping off my nose. We took off our tops and crawled up the grassy bank to the top of the red stone bunker at the very back, where it touched the tree line. We opened two beers to cool down in the shade. I always hated the first swig of beer, but it got easier; nice even, the more you drank. At least it was cold. Finn had packed them in with frozen peas to keep them chilled, which I would never have thought to do. We held the cold cans to our foreheads and smiled as the beer started to work. We stretched out in the thin line of shadow that the trees had cast on the bunker's mossy concrete roof and closed our eyes. The bunker rumbled beneath us as we banged our heels on the surface and listened for the echoes inside, like the voices of trapped soldiers, or something. I liked the quieter moments like that. Finn and I didn't always say that much to each other, but it didn't matter. Sometimes, when it was quiet like that, it was better even.

Neither of us knew exactly what the bunker was, really, but we agreed beyond a doubt that it must have been a World War Two bomb shelter built in case the Nazis stormed North Wales. Which they might have done, you don't know. They seemed to be pretty desperate to storm places. It was a big, square, redbrick structure, built into the grass banks at the edge of the field in one of the furthest meadows. There were grids on either side where you could just about see inside – but it was weird, because you could never get a clear picture and there was always an echoey dripping noise of water when you held your ear to the gap and listened. Our dads both said it was a disused water treatment point, but that made no sense to us. Why build it into the bank like that, so secure? For protection, that's why. It had to be something to do with the war.

By the time we'd finished our first can we'd started to get a bit giddy. We had even forgotten about the diary. We opened another can and shared it, then decided to have rolling races down the grass bank, sideways, to see who reached the bottom first. It was always a laugh doing that, because with all the beer and the spinning, you felt really drunk after just one go. Sometimes we would crash into each other halfway down and you just had to roll over the other one. You got each other's sweat on you, but it didn't matter. It was kind of a rule that you just kept going no matter what you crashed in to.

After the third go, we were knackered. We just lay at the bottom of the bank, in the long grass and sunshine, panting. I was wheezing a bit but I wasn't worried about an attack. Sometimes, you just knew it would pass. One big cloud moved across the sky overhead and to me it looked like a fat dog or a hippo or something, but I decided not to say that out loud. I felt all happy and relaxed and I didn't want to ruin the moment. That was until I looked over at Finn and noticed that he was staring off at nothing in that distant way he'd had when he'd been flinging those sticks.

Shall we read the diary? I said. It seemed like the only thing *to* say.

Finn agreed so we went back on top of the bunker and put our T-shirts back on. We grabbed his rucksack and went and sat at the far edge, where the wall was the tallest and our legs could dangle off the side. He took the diary out slowly, like it was precious or fragile or something, then looked at me really seriously.

"Just one page though, nay?" he said. "It's shady, otherwise."

I nodded, and he held the closed book out in front of me. I pointed to a bit that I thought was near the middle and Finn wedged his thumb into a gap between the pages to mark it. But he didn't open it yet. He was breathing very deeply and staring at the point where his thumb was stuck.

Suddenly, he snapped the book open and started reading in a loud, clear voice:

"12th of March 1995. How did I get here? I am stuck in this house, losing my strength. I'm trapped, bumping against these windows, like a bee in a flowerless world…"

He stopped as suddenly as he'd started and slammed the book closed. A choking sound blocked the words in his throat and his face bulged suddenly all red and puffy. He pulled back his arm and threw the diary into the field as far as he could. He stood up, went to the rucksack. He pulled out the cigarettes and started smoking one. He was smoking it furiously, puffing and puffing and pacing about, just looking at the ground.

"We shouldn't have done that," he said, his voice all low and growly but I couldn't see any tears. He was puffing out his cheeks every time he blew out smoke like an angry dragon or something. I was going to say that to him, because it looked funny, but I guessed it wasn't the time. We'll laugh about it later, I thought.

"We shouldn't have fuckin' done that," he said again. "Why did you make me?"

I didn't, I half-said, but he was still speaking over me.

"Why 'd you make me, eh? We've got no right. We shouldn'ta done it, nay?"

Okay, I said quietly. Sorry, I said, but he wasn't listening. He was just pacing up and down and sometimes punching himself in the thigh, with short, stabby punches. He looked a bit scary, to be honest. I thought it might be one of those moments where he went schitz, so I was careful not to say anything stupid. He jumped down from the bunker and went to where he'd thrown the diary. He picked it up and wiped it down on each side. He brought it back to the bunker and packed it away in the rucksack carefully. Everything he did was angry now and urgent.

"We've got to go," he said.

Why, there's still…

"I've got to get this back," he said, "I shouldn't have taken it."

I knew there wasn't any point in arguing, even if there was more beer and fags and so much of the day left. Finn had the final say in things. It was his rucksack, his beer and he was the one who'd picked me after all. I crumpled up my can sadly and threw it into the trees.

We pretty much marched all the way back. Finn wasn't talking at all anymore. I tried to tell him that it could have meant anything, like a poem or something, where the words don't really mean what they say but something different and clever that you have to work out. It could be she just really likes writing that stuff, I said, but Finn didn't say anything – I just watched as his face went red and his eyes started to get puffy and watery again, although he didn't actually cry. I don't think I ever saw Finn really cry.

By the time we got back to the village, I was wheezing pretty hard and covered in sweat. I was trying to keep it quiet because I didn't want to sound like a spaz to him. I hoped he hadn't noticed my stupid red face or the big rings of sweat round my T-shirt, but to be honest, he wasn't noticing anything about me anymore. We split off separately by the stile again, back where we'd started off from. I said, well see you tomorrow then, but Finn just said goodbye quietly without even looking up. He vaulted the stile and lifted one arm as a sort of wave as he strode on and up the hill. He lived up Penant Briar, on the estate, and me down in the bungalows on Pen-y-Rho. I kept looking behind as I walked slowly away. I wanted to see if he was looking back at all, but he just kept straight on with his head down, rucksack bobbing. He looks like a soldier on a mission, I thought, which is funny now, but anyway. When he was out of sight, I started to run home. I wanted to get back to my room before anyone in the village could see me cry.

That night I thought about Finn. I wondered what he was doing at home. Did he look at his mother differently that evening? Did he try to smile at her across the dinner table when he caught her eye? Could he even bring himself to look at her at all? Did he draft her a letter that started *Dear mum*, then scrub that out and start again, over and over. Did he sit down next to her and quietly take her hand, his chest tight, a panicked feeling rising up inside? I never asked him about it.

We grew distant that next school year and by the end of it you wouldn't have even called us mates, to be honest. We didn't hang out again the next summer or any after that. We never went back to the bunker, not together, anyway. I guess he probably went with other boys. Sometimes I saw him in the village and we'd just nod at each other quickly then look away. I never had another friend like him.

Years later, after we'd moved away like most did, I heard that he had joined the army. That's a good thing, if it's true. It was what he wanted. From what I hear, though, his parents stayed together, in that same house. They stayed in the village, even after everything with the mine closing, when it got really tough. They're still there, last I heard. It is amazing, really, what people can take.

Bad Mayo

Arjan Kapoor knew that he was being fired, but he was finding it hard to care. He had known that the day, this day, had been coming for some time. He was fully aware of how poor his recent performance had been. Every indicator, down. Every interaction, flat. But for some time, he had also been living with the knowledge that his job, a Telemarketing Sales Manager for Syston Systems, a Loughborough-based acoustics firm specialising in immersive sound solutions for home entertainment, lacked any real meaning.

When he arrived at the office each morning, which was easily accessed from either Derby Road to the north or the A6 to the south, he did not feel unhappy. This was not part of his problem. He was no more or less happy entering his workplace than he was entering, say, a fast food chain restaurant or municipal swimming pool or repurposed attic space for city centre living. It was just that he felt nothing at all. And he continued not to for as long as the day endured.

The office, which boasted an enviable town centre location between branches of Greenwoods Menswear and Carphone Warehouse, was split into four sections. Each section, roughly a quarter of the rectangular shaped, 260 square-metered open plan utility, represented a sales district: Loughborough North and West; Loughborough Central; Loughborough South and East; and Leicester. Arjan's section, Leicester, had traditionally been the most lucrative. It wasn't any more.

The office, which – in line with government advice – had been fully refitted with a state of the art, self-regulating, green-energy air-con system as recently as 2012, looked exactly like anyone bothering to imagine it would imagine it. Each section had five booths for the Section Manager and the four Sales Representatives, with each booth partitioned by easily movable, steel-case 'work-walls' and offering a small portion of desk space, a PC, a centrally networked headset phone hub and an ergonomically adjusted wheely chair. Arjan's job was to direct the team's focus, set goals, look at data, motivate and help create training opportunities, work with large profile customers or with customer complaints, analyse budgets and determine ways to streamline and improve the sales process. He hadn't really been doing that.

But this absence of professional application and resultant slump in performance represented only a fraction of Arjan's current problems. Because Arjan had started seeing things. Or rather, not seeing things. Unseeing them. It had been happening for a month or so. When he looked at anything that consisted of easily degradable biomass: documents, wooden furniture, human beings, for example, he couldn't help reducing the spatial profile he saw in front of him to the commensurate pile of dust that their eventual and inevitable disintegration would leave behind on planet Earth. A piece of paper equalling one thimble full or so. A large person: one standard vase's worth.

The piles he saw were not exact measurements. He was not a fucking scientist. He was a soon to be ex-Sales Manager. And his problems didn't end there. Flavour was departing too. His ability to taste things, anything, was going the way of all flesh, that is, fucking right off. This was a more recent development. He had first noticed it the previous week, at his father's house. He was tucking into his Abba's special: curried cottage pie, trying hard not to visualise the whole thing in tiny grey particles, when he noticed the coriander was missing.

"Abba?" he asked, "Why no coriander, huh?"

"You're joking right?" answered his father, reflexively. "The recipe never changes, bala. Plenty coriander in there, boy. But be my guest."

His father had then pushed a bowl of the freshly chopped herb across the table in his son's direction. Arjan had sprinkled it liberally over his mash and curried mince. He'd scooped a forkful into his mouth. Nothing. The flavour he knew so well, the flavour of his youth, was entirely absent. He dipped into the dish again and pinched a fat portion between his fingers, this time carpeting his plate with a blanket of green. He took a bite. Nada. Nichts. Zilch. Finally, he scooped up a near handful of bright green leaves and dropped them directly into his mouth. His father looked at him agog. Arjan munched down powerfully on the grassy gobful with focus and consternation, ignoring his father's slack-jawed protestation. He took care to grind and pulp the thicker stems between his violently masticating molars, leaving nothing to chance, hoping to release some sudden rush of fragrant recognition. But no. The goo he swallowed tasted as bland as his quarterly sales spreadsheets. There was something deeply wrong.

Within the space of seven days, this absence of flavour had spread to almost everything he consumed. Everything had the taste and texture of bad mayonnaise. This was particularly distressing, as mayonnaise had formerly been one of his favourite condiments. Pickled Onion Monster Munch were a kind of acid test. Their particular brand of gum sucking tartness had always been his go-to hangover cure. Now, cramming the alien maize forms into his horribly contorting mouth, snorting like a bull to activate his still functioning olfactory senses (that, as a clever boy, he knew played a far greater role in the sense of taste than his lumpen tongue), he got nothing. He didn't do anything about this. He just accepted it. He resigned himself to the fact that taste was a sense he seemed to have lost. Or nearly lost. He still got something from a glass of neat whiskey.

And it was hard to place exactly when all this had started, the losing things. There was the haunting image of the empty vending machine. It was there, in the corridor outside their office, to keep the bored and hungry workforce in essential snacks but had been left empty for months due to an unexplained and protracted supplier dispute. Arjan kept seeing its marshalled rows of spiralled steel. The image, beautiful in its own hopeless way, would flash into his mind then disappear; if that didn't happen for a day or two, he would have to walk out into the corridor to stand and blandly stare at it a while. Regimented, precise, its chrome uniformity stood calibrated and coiled waiting diligently to dispense… nothing. Then there had been those pictures of his colleague's Chihuahua that had made him feel angry and nauseous. Or the conference in Coventry where the pin from a delegate's name badge had skewered him square in the fleshy thumb tip, but instead of recoiling from the flatly registered pain, he'd had the urge to just keep pushing and pushing until the point of the pin burst bloodily through the fissured thumbnail above.

Of course, none of this was easily explained to a man like Mr. Fensteterine. Mr. Fensteterine was his boss and not only did he have a name that sounded like a prescription-only mouth wash, but he possessed the personal qualities to match. Always well turned out and aggressively fresh, he liked his employees to reflect his *ethos* in every possible way. He liked SMART targets and PowerPoint presentations. He liked to 'work hard and play hard', and he liked to tell people that that was what he liked. He did not like conversations about emotions or outcomes that were hard to quantify. In short, he was a prick.

Mr. Fensteterine had already had Pauline Atack, his unfortunately named and hideously dressed head of HR, draft, edit and send two written warnings pertaining to Arjan's worrying slump in performance. Arjan had opened, glanced at and binned these missives in two near identical movements without sending any form of response to his manager. There were currently close to forty unopened emails in his inbox labelled URGENT too. When he was finally called into Mr. Fensteterine's glass partitioned office, which doubled as a conference space in order to demonstrate the management´s own commitment to a recently introduced *hot-desking* arrangement, he was in no doubt as to why he was there.

He pushed open the door and entered the room. The sweet, frigid wash of the air-con swept over him as the door behind clunked shut under its own weight. There were three people sitting across the large fake mahogany desk in front of him. He knew two of them. Mr Fensteterine sat centrally; Pauline Atack was to his right. To his boss's left, the right of the room as Arjan looked at it, was a man he had never seen before. The man seemed to be sitting an unnecessary distance from Mr. Fensteterine, perhaps to denote observer status. Legal, Arjan guessed, a presumption which represented the sum total of his curiosity. Nobody stood to greet Arjan when he entered, but Mr. Fensteterine did gesture to the vacant seat in front of them with one of his long straight arms and a flat, pink palm, so Arjan sat.

The room smelt of cloying, floral perfume and a faint trace of minted cough sweet, both the fault of Ms. Atack. Arjan couldn't understand why his sense of smell remained just as keen as ever when his sense of taste had been so completely obliterated. It didn't make sense. Another bad joke. He hated the smell of Pauline's perfume, which dominated the office even when she wasn't around, but perhaps, he reasoned, this process worked in stages and eventually smell would go too. He doubted, however, that such a mercy would transpire before the end of their meeting. He was unlikely to get that lucky.

Within a second or so of Arjan taking his seat, Mr. Fensteterine began talking. Arjan straightened up in his seat instinctively and tried to focus on Mr. Fensteterine's flapping, big toothed, clapper-board mouth. He could hear the words that were spoken. In reality they went:

"Mr. Kapoor, Arjan, I think you know why we are here today..."

But in his mind, they went:

"EEEEwwwwrrrrrgggghhhhhhhhhhhhh.   Blah. Blleerruuugghghghghghghggghghhghghghghghh. Blurgh. Blurgh. Blurgh."

Then it started to happen, just as he'd expected. Mr Fensteterine's lips frosted silver at their edges before turning entirely grey. For just a fleeting moment, it gave the impression that Mr. Fensteterine was wearing a kind of futuristic lipstick. "Maybe it's Maybeline?" thought Arjan, and this was enough to make him smile. This in turn triggered a remark from his boss about the gravity of the situation, which then made Ms. Atack nod furiously, but Arjan barely registered this because he was watching Mr. Fensteterine's whole head turn grey and pixely.

Mr. Fensteterine's grey pixel-head was saying something about legal obligations by the time it started to degenerate. The pixels, particles, or whatever they were exactly, started to descend from their bodied origin and decamp into a pile on the desk in front of them. The particles shrank as they went and each particle followed precisely after the last, like watching a pack of computerised Solitaire cards reorder themselves on your PC monitor when you have invariably lost patience and started a new game. Where they gathered on the desk, they made the customary grey pile that Arjan had become used to. The pile was quite large as Mr. Fensteterine had been a tall man and his voice continued to be projected from the centre of the pile. The two other interviewers remained completely unmoved and temporarily whole, nodding or not nodding at intervals. Pauline's flared, garish green floral blouse blared at Arjan like a furious emerald goose, honking at him from the corner of his eye, which made it even harder to concentrate on what the pile of Mr. Fensteterine was saying. "I really could do with a drink," thought Arjan. He licked his dry lips.

There was a bar, *New York, New York*, that was just down the street from the office. Arjan started to picture it now. It was not the one his colleagues drank at, which was exactly why he went there. It was a bit of a dive, with dirty stools by the dirty black bar and black walls where busted florescent strip lighting hung in an apparently random configuration. He often wondered about who had put the lighting there and why. What exactly could they have intended with that arrangement? What he liked most, though, was the set of broken clocks that clung to the wall behind the bar, telling the time incorrectly in three different time zones. New York, London, Tokyo: all out by a decent margin. He liked the idea of that. Categorically wrong in three different time zones. The sense of it sang to him, siren-like, from the dreary high street.

Back in Mr. Fensteterine's office, Pauline Atack was pushing a quickly pixelating form and a ball point pen across the table, presumably for Arjan to authorise his own dismissal. Arjan tried to look in Pauline's direction and acknowledge her or the moment, but she was breaking up too. Arjan smiled weakly. His eyes filled with tears, although he could not tell if he really felt like crying. Ms. Atack's voice sounded calmer, more cajoling than Mr. Fensteterine's, but that didn't stop her face, limbs, and body crumbling to grey dust and piling themselves up on the dark wood table top.

Arjan wiped a forefinger along the length of each eye and tried to compose himself, but suddenly he felt that his tie was very tight around his throat. He coughed. He poked a finger into the knot and started loosening it. It felt good to let some of the cool air in, so he loosened it further. He noticed as he did this that the only other still-whole person in the room, the silent adjudicator or whatever the fuck he was, instinctively put his hand to his throat too. "People just do things, automatically, without thinking," thought Arjan. This meeting was an example. He stood up. Pauline Atack's pile of grey matter was making noise in an increasingly higher pitch, but Arjan's mind was now entirely occupied by the idiocy of ties. He took his off and dropped it. It was pixel bits before it hit the floor. He strode over to the sanctioned interloper. He held out his hand. He wanted to do this one thing before the man became dust too. He stood there, trembling, for a number of seconds, his hand out, until this man he did not know at all reached across the desk and shook it.

The Stepdaughter

Today, if she has been counting right, must be a Thursday, which means, yes, that's right, it could be today. Last night, she thinks it was last night, or maybe in the afternoon? Not that it matters, not that any of it matters… but she thought she had heard that tough nurse say,

"It's *always* Jell-O on Wednesdays, Alice, you *know* that."

And she thought, well that's just typical of that blessed meanie, but she also thought, make a note, Alice. Make a note. Wednesday. That means just one more day.

She´s either scared or she´s worried. The fear just lingers, always, fogging everything, but in her clearer moments, like now, sitting here, waiting, she worries how she'll recognise the girl. Sight has left her, gone entirely now, sometime in the last month. So she will no longer see the girl, that much is certain. She won't be allowed to touch her either of course. Let alone hold her. Let alone drink her in, bodily. Let alone smell her.

Oh, how nice that was. Smelling someone. Knowing someone by their smell. The faint, ghost-oil scent of someone you love: on the bedsheets, their discarded clothes, on you. Edward isn't the same. He stinks, god bless him, the messy christer, though she's past telling him. All those cigarettes. No, they've told her quite clearly, the people here: no touching.

Will I even remember her voice? She asks herself. It was a beautiful, strong, clear voice. Can she bring it to mind now if she tries? No. No, that's gone too. But the smile remains. That beaming smile she had. What was her name again? Something French. From that strange bloody father. Therese. That's it! Beautiful Therese. She only ever thinks of her as The Girl.

It has kept her company these slowly blinding years, that smile. Things come and go, but that has stayed. It has lit her days and haunted her nights in this place, high up on the hill, where she'd come to die. She'd been ready to do it, too. As the world around her lost its memory, then went mad and then, finally, receded into black, she could close her eyes and see that smile. She had been content with it. Content to hold the memory, that alone, and let go of all the rest. But recently, a frightened urgency has taken over her; a tremor where a heartbeat should be, in the rattling, hollow cage of her chest. Three women in the floor above died, one after the other, in the space of a week. Then they changed the rules about visitors and even Edward, her only son, stopped coming for a while. They said he was a risk to her. To all of them. They said everyone was a risk now. She was scared. She had thought herself ready for it, however it came, so she hadn't expected to feel *this* frightened. The last patches of light faded quickly. That smile, the memory of it, was fading too. She felt trapped and alone and she only wanted to see The Girl.

The Girl, Therese, had come into Alice's life when she had all but given up hope of a grandchild. She was seventy years old when Edward, who had seemed destined to live his life a bachelor, met the girl's mother and married quickly. Too quickly. Therese's mother, Caroline, had been too hasty by half. She should have checked Edward out. Lived with him first, the messy christer. Done at least a little research. But she had wanted a father for the child, that's what Alice guessed – by God, she could understand it – and she had decided that Edward would do.

If she had asked, Alice could have told her hasty daughter-in-law to tread carefully. Her son, God love him, was a strange man. Growing up in that woody suburb. Just the two of them, which was nobody's fault. He had strange habits. Phone calls he would only take in the basement and such nonsense. Noises from his 'office'. She could have told her to be strict. The things to look out for and what they meant. The things she should not allow. But they were both grown adults and there was a child involved and they were way past asking anyone's opinion. So, it ended the way it did: badly.

Ed had told her not to get her hopes up. He said, with everything the way it was, probably not. He himself had barely seen the girl in the years since the separation. Wasn't *allowed*. Once or twice at Christmas. Once or twice in how long? Five years now? Ten? Alice was ninety years old. Good god, it had been ten years! That was just as long as the marriage had lasted.

Ten short years they had been a family. Not a happy one, no, you couldn't honestly say that. Caroline and Edward argued from the start and never really did get settled on one another – bedroom trouble, as if anyone had asked or couldn't have guessed, but by Christ the way she went on. She let the whole world know about it. His *deficiencies*, as she termed them. It stank. Anyway, because of that, all the fighting, Alice and Therese had become a kind of a team. The Ignorami, they called themselves, ironically, after one of Edward's silly rants. They had the simple goal of keeping each other sane through all of the shouting and banging of doors and the mundane, painful silences.

They did more than that, though. They became friends. It had delighted Alice not just to remember, but to relive, through Therese, the bewildering excitement of girlhood. It was like getting a fresh go at it all. The bloody wonder of pulling teeth you knew would grow back. The joy of a cold pop by the lake in Irishtown on a sunny Saturday. Playing at horses, then riding horses, then living for those gosh darned horses right up until the boys came along. Ha! And they came along, all right! She was a beauty, the girl. When they met, Therese was just seven years old. By the time they left she was nearly a woman. It really had been something.

They all lived over in Moncton then, before Caroline took her divorce money and Therese over to the Big Smoke and left Edward somehow sadder and lonelier than when they'd started out. Ten years she had been a grandmother, in the legal and every other gosh darned sense to that child. She had bathed her, clothed her, cooked for her. Ten years and then suddenly, whoosh, she is nothing to do with you anymore. Human beings are such strange creatures. The fictions they fashion are so powerful. Barriers and bonds built out of nothing but feelings, words, maybe something as flimsy as a document, but you just see how once some door slams shut inside, they're impenetrable and cold as stone. Ed had said not to get her hopes up, what with the situation and everything, but he had got a message to the girl anyhow. Against all odds, she was coming to visit.

***

It had not been a surprise when Edward contacted her. From the moment the lockdown had started, Therese's thoughts had turned to her lonely stepfather and his lonelier mother, out there on the hill, in Shediac. She had wondered more than once in the past two months how Alice was doing, if she was still alive, even, so in a way, the message came as a relief. It made her sad to think of that beautiful, bright old lady who had always been so full of spark, sputtering out somewhere without anyone other than Edward to hold her hand. He loved his mother, sure. Loved her in a strangely close, strangely grudging way, but he had never been good with those kinds of things. Emotional things. When the email had dropped in her inbox, she'd barely needed to think about it. She'd put down a box of files and papers. The office, which had been nigh on empty for days, was eerie quiet. She was collecting her things, fixing to be gone for a fair few months herself. So, she'd read the short message and written back immediately.

"Of course, I will come," she had written, "it will be good to see you both."

That wasn't entirely true, of course. Therese *wanted* to see Alice. Even more so now, reading between the lines of Edward's clipped but passively pleading prose. She had always loved to see Alice, but it had long since stopped being especially *good* to see her adoptive father. Putting all the bad memories aside, and there were a few, Edward was a mess. His smoking, his drinking, his strange undiagnosed eating disorders, they'd all been bad when he'd been with her mother, but he'd since let them get out of control. He was now painfully thin. Upsettingly so, felt Therese, though she hated herself to admit it. He had open sores on his legs that never fully healed and he stank to high heaven. The home he'd inherited from Alice, the one Therese had once called home too, was a dilapidated mess. She figured she'd have to spend at least one night there, so as not to hurt his feelings. Last time she'd visited, she'd slept on a sheetless mattress on the sticky floor. She'd had to lay down her own towels and sleep with one wrapped around her face, fearful to breathe too deep and surrounded by the fine layer of ash that had settled on everything in the decade they'd been gone. But she packed some bedding this time and booked the flight anyway. Montreal to Moncton. A four hundred dollar round trip. It was expensive and somewhat against the guidance but, she factored sadly, what the heck.

***

When she lands in the pale light of the early afternoon, everything brings her close to tears. The familiar route through the outskirts of the city, over junctions, past turn offs and the reasons she used to take them. The shake joint near the freeway where she'd met that boy called Freddie on her first real date. Where could he be now, Freddie? That bunch of yellowed pine tree air fresheners hanging from the rear-view mirror of Edward's beat up gold Mazda that she guesses are the same ones from way back when. It is all too much. She knows it is probably hormonal. She has expected as much and she has made herself ready. Practiced exactly what she needs to do. When she lands, she asks him, Edward, Ed, the man she had once awkwardly learned to call Dad, to take her straight there, straight to Alice.

He tells her he can't. There is a slot. They only give out one slot, these days, because of the virus. One hour. Alice's is at four p.m. One visitor allowed per resident per day, maximum. And this is almost enough to make her burst into tears, right there in arrivals, but she stops herself, gathers herself, dries her eyes. They head to a roadside coffee stop on the 134 to drink decaf and talk about their jobs.

It is quiet and almost empty in the diner. Therese looks around for anything she might remember, but the place is strange to her. She says, so, where to start, and puts a hand to her stomach without thinking, but Ed is ordering the coffee and doesn't notice. So, she says, she is a Social Worker now, like him. Yeah, go figure, right? I mean, naturally. He laughs and, seeing this, she softens a bit. It is nice to see him smile. They both laugh a while, before it goes quiet again. Little coughs catch in their dry throats.

The waitress arrives and pours a little coffee into each of their cups. She puts down the pot on the table and leaves. To fill the silence Ed gets to talking about some of his recent cases. It's his old go-to. He tells her, as he always liked to do, about the tough kids: *hard cases*, as he calls them, the ones who are always the smartest in their own sad way, and she remembers what a good talker he is and how full of compassion for strangers, and how chats just like this one most likely led her to the job that she does now. She smiles again.

He smokes, though, she guesses, less than he would do normally, ducking outside at intervals for some hurried pulls, then returning and picking up the conversation right where he left it. She lets him drive the talk, because it's easier that way, it's what he does, what she lets him do and always has, but she has to stop him twice. She has to stop him when he wants to stray on to his relationship with her mother, to portion out the blame again, because she won't let him do that. Says she can't handle that too. Not today. Not anymore, in fact. Everything has been said too many times already. It is time everyone moved on. And she is strong on this in a way she hasn't been before, and he senses that. Respects it. Backs down. So they talk about other things, silly things, anything else in fact, even about his goddamned ice hockey team, which she used to hate to do, but now it's fine somehow, if a little forced, until he says,

"Okay, come on, it's time. I'll take you over."

***

She fills out the forms at the front desk, but she doesn't write anything other than *granddaughter* because she doesn't want to complicate matters. She just wants to see Alice one last time and that is all. When they let her into the room it is dark and lit by just one small lamp. Therese wants to ask why no one has thought to put the big light on but then she remembers and holds her tongue. Alice is huddled over by the window, swaddled into a wheelchair by a thick shawl of blankets, her little white head tilted sideward towards the pale afternoon light. She looks so small.

"Hello Alice," she says, and smiles as she sees the small ripple of timid joy register in the shrunken woman's wrinkled face.

"Oh, hello, my love. Is it you?" Alice asks, nervously, instinctively tilting her face in the general direction of the door.

"It's me. It's Therese," she says and she pulls a chair over, positions it the 1.5 metres from Alice's wheelchair, the distance she's been told she must hold, and sits. It hurts not to go to Alice. Not to go to her old friend and take her in her arms feels wrong.

"Brought you a Coffee Crisp. I remember how you liked those, " says Therese, holding out the yellow wrapped candy in front of her, then, as it hangs a little too long in the air, feeling stupid and withdrawing it again.

"I don't know," says Alice. Her voice is small too. Everything in this room seems diminished.

"Well, that's ok. I'll just put it right here on your dresser. How you been? Not too hot, huh?" Asks Therese, trying her best to sound normal, but terrified of what the old lady will say, choking up when she sees how every syllable she speaks seems to light sparks in Alice's eyes. They strain and narrow at the sounds, as if trying to read passing signs through thick fog.

"Oh, not good," Alice, says. "Been forgetting things, you know. Days, months. I forget the names. But you're here now so that's good. I been waitin'. What did you say your name was again?"

"Therese," says Therese and smiles. Alice was always the most intelligent, sharpest person she knew. She'd read God knows how many books. Followed the news. Always switched on. When they'd met, she was already seventy and was still sharper than a paper cut. Full of energy, too. More intelligent than any of the many teachers she'd met in any of her many schools and far, far more fun. They had played together, joked together, and Alice never seemed to tire. Therese had met many *grandparents* over the years – but they were old folks. Alice, she had often thought, got older – but never old. Until now.

"Yes, yes. Therese. The Girl. Caroline's girl." The old lady smiles. "Is Ed there?"

"Edward is outside. He will see you again tomorrow, OK? It is just us today."

"Oh yes, that's fine," says Alice. "Poor old Edward. They say he's a risk, eh? Everyone's a gosh darned risk. We mustn't go too close. I don't know..."

The way the old lady's voice trails off makes Therese ache. She looks around the room. It is a nice, small, but painfully temporary space; austere, but not uncomfortable. There are pictures of Edward, a picture of herself aged sixteen, grinning awkwardly from behind a horrendous fringe, and some very old, age-browned photos of people she does not know, but vaguely recalls from the house in Moncton. There are no pictures of Therese's mother, which is understandable. She tries to think of something she can do for the old lady without physical contact. There are some books on her bedside table that have probably lain there undisturbed for quite some time. "I could read to her," she thinks, but then she is distracted by a burst of breaking sunlight in the garden outside. Opposite Alice's window there is a single tree, a ginkgo, in the middle of a large, lush lawn. It is suddenly framed in beautiful fall sunshine, an almost supernatural yellow, like the spirit of a tree breaking through from wherever it is tree spirits reside. Therese can barely believe it.

"Hey," she says, "do you know this tree right here?"

Alice pauses. A tree? She can't remember a tree. Can't remember zip about any garden. Therese senses immediately how this distresses her.

"Well never mind, honey, but she sure is a beauty. How's about I describe her for you, eh? She's a beauty, just like you."

Alice nods and Therese begins. She tells Alice that the tree outside her window, the tree she has forgotten, is as big as a brown bear over a bee hive, but gold like a lion in the savannah sun. She describes how the branches fan proudly to each side, open armed, as though inviting the embrace of the whole gosh-darned world and how the leaves, tickled by the slightest autumn breeze, glow from the inside out, bursting with radiant, defiant colour before the coming of mean old winter. She smiles as she explains how this tree, this one alone, is like its own brash flag of independence and it could only look this way from just this angle at just this time, capturing the light that bounces off of Alice's little window, that flows out from Alice herself, making the world around her brighter just by being there. And as Therese talks she smiles. And as Therese is smiling, Alice hears that familiar grin, the joyful stretching of sinews, carried on the slightest uplift of her voice. She hears the words bending upwards out of her pretty mouth, their concave curves and upward undulation, like the stalks of a sun seeking plant, twisting, reaching for the light just like that radiant ginkgo. And quite instead of that ginkgo, the one that Therese is taking such care to describe, Alice sees The Girl smiling in her mind's eye and it is beautiful. So beautiful that she begins to weep.

Therese stops. She puts a hand to her mouth as though she has somehow said too much. She tries, soundlessly, to gather herself, swallow the lump in her throat, hold back her own tears that suddenly threaten to flood the moment. The distance between them, small though it is, feels awful. She remembers how much Alice loved to be touched, to be massaged and held, to be kneaded and fussed – all those years without a lover – all those years without a child – and because of this, despite herself, Therese feels herself rising from her seat. It is not meant as an act of rebellion, for she is not really thinking at all. She is just reacting to Alice's awful isolation; the simple need to be touched. Because who could resist so human a need? "Not me," she says, inside. Not now.

"Alice, I'm going to touch you now, honey, OK? I know the rules, but I been real safe on my way over and, and… I won't if you don't wanna, but I think you need a hug. Is that OK?"

"Oh yes," says Alice, sniffing through the tears, "Oh, yes, yes please."

Therese stands, and walks around the back of Alice's chair. She leans down, puts her head next to Alice's, she kisses her on her cold cheek and gently wraps her long arms around the old lady's frail chest.

When Alice feels the warmth of the girl's strong embrace around her shoulders, she nuzzles into the crook of the young woman's neck where her sleek auburn hair hangs about her face. She breathes in deeply. She smells the same. Like then: petals and buttermilk. How can that be? The seven-year-old kid. The Girl. She has come back.

"Oh," says Alice, with a whimper, then she cries again. And it is much harder this time. Not a trickle, now. A dam breaks. Her fragile body shakes with the sobs. Therese tells her it´s okay. She tells her to let it all out. She rubs her shoulders and pats her back gently.

When she has finished crying and dried her tears, Alice asks Therese to hold her hand while she says a prayer. It is a strange thing to do, the old lady knows. She says she never believed before, but these days, in the dark, she finds she needs… something. She doesn't know if it will do any good, she says, since she never went to church and she isn't even halfway sure which God she has in mind, really. That's alright, says the girl. It's okay not to know. Remember our club? Can you remember, Alice? The Ignorami? We can both not know together. Like back then. Like always.

So they say the prayer. Therese goes back to rubbing Alice's shoulders as they try to put it together, this half-remembered prayer. Alice forgets how it goes. She leaves bits out. They both do, at times, they make mistakes. "Our father," they say, anyway. Forgive us our trespasses. Deliver us from evil. And then, when it is over, they are silent for a while. And they allow that too. Silently holding on, though every once in a while, Alice starts and reaches up a hand to feel for one or two of Therese's slim fingers, as if to check she is still there. Therese wiggles them, to let her know she is. The deft hour passes this way: still and warm, all too quick. At last, a nurse knocks gently on the door to signal time.

And that is it. It has to be. The rules say it is time to go and there are some rules you don't get to choose. So, Therese stoops down, puts her arms around Alice once more, and whispers in her ear again.

"You've been the best gosh darned Grandma a girl could have," she tells her, and she means it.

She kisses the old lady softly on the crown of her head. She cradles her head and then holds it to her warm, round belly and she kisses it again. It's a long kiss this time. Years are in it. The ones that they've had together and all the ones apart. And as her head rests on the rounded curve of the girl's taut skin, Alice thinks she hears something inside. And she recognises it. She knows it, yes, she knows it of old! That heartbeat – like the one she'd thought she'd lost. Tiny and quick; strong and clear. They hold each other, these women, and they cry. Both of them. All of them. Together.

The Day the Jehovahs Came

Ray was not looking for God the day the Jehovahs came. Ray had been not looking for God for quite some time. That day, a Tuesday, Ray had to get through all those things he had not done Monday. Monday, he had spent the whole day drunk.

So, on this Tuesday, instead of looking for God, Ray was thinking of how he would need to ditch those magazines he could not sell with that guy Richard. How he had to make it to the bank and see about another extension, then scour the jobs section in the local rag for anything: unskilled, part time, anything. How he had to hit the shops, stop in at the bookies, feed the cats, feed himself, wash the dishes, clean the flat. And all the while with that dull ache from the weekend in his face and ribs nagging at him to take it easy. Lie down, for fuck's sake. Take it easy.

Ray might not have even opened the door to God had his anointed people not been so persistent with the apartment buzzer. He really didn't have the time. He was rushed off his feet. But after the third or fourth rasping call, he picked himself up off the sofa and at the press of a button, let the Jehovahs, God and all, into the building.

Of course, Ray did not know the people were Jehovahs until he opened the door to his apartment and saw what looked like a pair of anaemic sales reps standing there. They were dressed in white shirts and pleated black pants. One woman, one man. They looked like clones. Not twins, but clones. The only way to tell them apart was that one had long straight blond hair and the other's was blond but cropped tight. The female clone had a very flat chest. They were both quite young and wore black rimmed glasses. To Ray, they looked more like Mormons, or the Mormons of his imagination, but he'd already clocked the literature clasped conspicuously close to their hearts. Watchtower. Shit.

They smiled big, blonde, blue-eyed smiles – smiles that started at the tips of their black, polished shoes and just kept going up. Hallelujah, Ray thought, as the boy clone asked whether Ray had put any thought into why the Bible might be important for people in the world today.

"No," Ray replied, "and I am not interested."

He stepped back and began to close the door on the two clones, but the female one, who apparently had some guts inside her, moved forward quickly to obstruct him, nudging a polished shoe-tip inside the door frame, and asked snappily:

"Sir, might I ask what happened to your eye?"

Ray had almost forgotten about the thing from Sunday night. Almost forgotten about the jagged line of scruffy-looking stitches above his left eyebrow that had kind of kick-started this latest binge. Instinctively, he brought his hand up and dabbed the area sorely.

"Oh…that. It's nothing. Just an accident. That's all."

"Sir…" the girl continued "Wouldn't you *please* just take one of these? You might find something in there that can help you. There are details of where to find us on the back."

Ray looked down and the girl was holding a flier in front of him with some large black writing across the front. **Why Read the Bible?** it said. He looked back up at the girl, whose blue eyes seemed to flicker and plead a little, and thinking 'what harm can it do?' he took the flier from her hand with a nod. She smiled again, seeming satisfied, and stepped back from the door. Ray closed it and went back inside.

He walked into the kitchen and looked at the pile of dishes in the sink. On one of the plates at the top of the pile there had formed a greenish-grey encrusted stain around the outer rim. Why did this happen to old dishes? It didn't seem related to any of the food he'd eaten lately. He could not for the life of him remember what he might have consumed that would leave such a stain, but there it was. He put the flier down idly on the kitchen table.

His two cats, one black and one white, had disappeared again. They were disappearing more regularly these days and for longer periods of time. It didn't worry him that much. Ray did not mind cats, but he did not trust them. He had inherited these two after his most recent break up. A nasty one. He stayed put in the flat, he'd been there first, and when she moved out, she just left them behind. Heartless bitch.

Ray had always known that cats were incredibly self-serving creatures. They had no sense of loyalty, when it came down to it. He didn't blame them for that, he understood nature fairly well, he thought, but it was cold comfort. He knew well enough that if they did not come back, it was only because they had found a better deal elsewhere. He closed the kitchen window that looked on to the courtyard. There was a lot to get through that day, so he put on his coat and left the flat.

***

When Ray returned that evening and entered the hallway of his apartment, he could make out a high-pitched whining noise coming from the kitchen. He stepped in. There they were, the cats, pawing at the windowpane and complaining to be let inside. He made a small sound in his throat, something between a cough and a laugh. "Little shits," he murmured, as he set his shopping down on the table and opened the slimmest crack in the window. The cats squeezed and scampered through then began circling their food bowl restlessly, all the while emitting the same impatient squeal he had heard coming from outside. It made his head hurt.

"You greedy little pricks…" he started to say, aloud, but it occurred to him then that he had not actually fed the animals for a week or more, so he quickly clawed open two cans of cat food and tipped it all out into one bowl. There.

He then started unpacking his shopping. Into the freezer he put a box of strawberry ice cream cones, but not before removing one and placing it on the table. Something for now. Into the fridge he put a bottle of lemonade, three bottles of milk and a tub of margarine. In the bread bin he placed a sliced white loaf. Finally, he unloaded six bottles of red wine, laying them out in a row on the table in front of him. Then he sat down.

He stared flatly at the bottles without blinking. He appeared for all the world like a grand master contemplating a devastating chess move. He felt the rumbling of that familiar excitement. Like a hard on, but internal, pushing inward, up into his guts. His eyes started to move hungrily backwards and forwards over the different labels. Embossed decoration; %vol.; wine makers´ names. He sat there and did not move his gaze from them, except once, when his eyes flicked quickly back to the washing up that was waiting in the sink. After a while he let out a deep sigh, as though some decision had been arrived at, and scrunched up the empty shopping bags into tight little balls in his fists. When he did this the Jehovah flier, which had been silently lurking beneath the plastic bags, flicked up off the table top, and fluttered down to rest at his feet. Ray threw the balled plastic bags in the direction of the large, overflowing garbage can in the corner of the room and stooped to pick up the flier. *Why Read the Bible?* it asked. It struck him as a good question.

He sat down at the table and laid the flier out flat. It folded out into three parts. He picked up the ice cream he had set aside and started to remove the packaging. He contemplated the pretty pictures on the flier, which showed grown men playing with lambs and a Chinese woman chatting to a Caucasian child who held a fruit basket. Everyone in the pictures smiled inanely at one another as though in the grip of some euphoric drug. He laughed a little at the funny pictures without grasping, or caring about, what they were supposed to mean.

At that point, suddenly, though without any noticeable celestial provocation, Ray decided to strike a deal with God. Gripped by an unforeseen and only slightly mocking seriousness, Ray explained to God that he would read this flier, but – and this was his one unique and important criterion – only for the time it took him to eat his ice cream. If Ray's attention was held after the ice cream was finished – if he wanted to read on – then God had won the contest and Ray might concede that maybe-just-maybe there was more *out there* than the he'd reckoned with so far. Maybe, even, he would look up the Jehovah Clones´ Bible class and check it out. Get into nodding sagely and clapping and proclaiming the lord, all that crap. But if Ray was bored by the flier, if he did not *want* to read on once he had eaten his Cornetto, then God was banished for ever and Ray would expect never to be bothered again. Ray took his first lick of the cone. The tasty little contest began.

Why Read the Bible?

The Bible is unlike any other book – it contains loving instruction from God. (1 Thessalonians 2:13). If you apply what the Bible teaches, you will benefit greatly. You will increase your love for God and draw him close to you, the Giver of "every good gift and every perfect present" (James 1:17). You will come to know how to approach him in prayer. During times of trouble…

Eating ice creams always made Ray think of his childhood,

back when he was a really small kid. It was probably why he kept buying them, this particular brand, because of their similarity to the ones from those days, out at the lake, when his parents had seemed to be sort of happy. He would sit there, his feet dangling over the side of the jetty, milky circles spreading in the water below as they laughed and teased each other or splashed in the shallows. There was always sunshine then. All that picture book shit.

He had stopped reading quite accidentally and now he gazed deeply into the bright, red sorbet crown as it melted and melded with the softer pink colours of the ice cream beneath. He made grooved rings in the top with his tongue, the way he'd perfected back in the day. The cats were circling his feet. Perhaps they were still hungry and hoped that some of the melted cream would drip down from his hand, onto the floor. Maybe they just wanted some attention. He played games with the cats, making shapes in the air above their heads with the cornet so that they followed excitedly. He licked his lips and looked over at the wine again. He shook his head slowly – the ice cream was melting in his hand and he was aware that he was cheating the deal he'd made with the Lord. Ray was a slow reader and that didn't give God much time to put his message across. He had to give God a fair chance, so he tried to focus, and he read on:

During times of trouble, you can experience God's help. If you harmonise your life with the standards set out in the Bible, God will give you everlasting life. (Romans 6:23).

The Bible contains truths that give enlightenment. Those who gain Bible knowledge are liberated from the misconceptions that dominate the lives of millions. For example, knowing the truth about what happens when we die frees us from the fear that the dead can harm us or that our dead relatives and friends are suffering (Ezekiel 18:4).

Ray stood sharply and strode over to the sink. The green stained plate was in his eye line and he could not concentrate.

He forced it down beneath the lip of the basin and then sat down again. He had only eaten the top part of his cone, but so far God was trailing badly. The flier read like the deranged gabbling of a mental patient. God, though, still had the ice cream filled cone part and the chocolate chunk at the bottom to catch up. Ray picked up the flier again, angrily.

"Okay," he said. "Come on."

The Bible's teaching of the resurrection gives comfort to those who have lost loved ones in death. (John 11:25) Knowing the truth about wicked angels alerts us to the dangers of spiritism and helps us to understand why there is so much trouble on earth.

Between paragraphs, Ray could not help looking up at the wine laid out before him. It seemed to him now like a prize. If he could just get God out of the room, he would be alone with his prize. Every time he looked up, the cut above his left eye itched and ached. He felt a throbbing sensation there too, where the stitches worked themselves spitefully against the swollen, purple flesh. He took another bite of his cone. What he read next almost made him spit it out.

The godly principles in the Bible show us how to live in a way that brings physical benefits. For example, being 'moderate in habits' contributes to good health. (Timothy 3:12)

"Pah…You don't say!" thought Ray. It was amazing to him that people could buy this kind of common sense bullshit as if it were the true word of God. He wondered what the Jehovah Clones were hoping to achieve, handing out such crap. Was anyone ever won over by this garbage? It simply couldn't be. He had less than half a cone left in one hand, and God's message in the other. It wasn't even close. God really needed a miracle, but a deal's a deal, he thought, so on he went.

Applying God's counsel found in the bible also promotes happiness in marriage and self-respect. If you apply God's word, you will be a happier person. Bible knowledge helps us to find inner peace and contentment and gives us hope. It helps us to cultivate such appealing qualities as compassion, love, joy, peace, kindness and faith. (Galatians 5:22; Ephesians 4:24) Such qualities help to make us a better husband or wife, father or mother, son or daughter.

It struck Ray, bitterly, that none of these categories could be meaningfully said to encompass him. Not anymore. He knew then for sure that he could not be *saved*. God had reached out with a fistful of umbrella terms, but still he had slipped through that almighty grasp. Ray had read only two columns of the pamphlet, but he was about done. It hardly seemed to matter that there was one bite of the cone left to go. He swallowed it at the same time as he read the heading above the third and final column: "*Are you willing to spend some time each week to learn the Bible?*"

Ray stood, shook his head once more, then deposited the crumpled pamphlet in the bin. It sat there forlornly, crackling slightly on top of the plastic bags. He strolled over to the sink and, triumphantly, he pulled out the drawer containing the corkscrew. He uncorked the first of the bottles and poured himself a very tall glass of very cheap Merlot. At last. God was gone, and all that was left was the blood of his only son. In the night to come he'd make short work of that, too. He laughed dryly at that thought. The fridge buzzed. The room was otherwise quiet and still.

The cats had disappeared again, he noticed. They'd slipped out of the window and into the night, little pricks. Ray wasn't worried. They'd come back again in time. If they didn't, then it was only because they'd found a better deal someplace else. And who on earth could blame them for that?

To Lie with Dogs

(*Forsooth*) the most remarkable comeback of any carnivore in Europe is that of the Eurasian wolf (*Canis lupus lupus*). In some, (*nobler*) areas of Europe there have resided stable populations of this (*most majestic*) grey wolf subspecies, but a long history of hunting and persecution *(man-us cunticus)* meant that by the first half of the twentieth century the animal had disappeared from most Western European countries *(shame, shame, know your name).*

"Zeppelin! Boardroom 3. Now!"

Zeynep Kopek likes to read about wolves at work. She is very much into wolves. Other animals too, but mainly wolves. She likes to visit websites like rewilding-europe.com or National Geographic or even, if she is feeling particularly bristly, an Otherkin or Therian forum, just to really lap it all up. Go wild (*tee hee*). She has developed a habit of mentally annotating any bland sections of text with her own internally italicised additions to render the information more accurate or interesting or… whatever. It calms her. She particularly likes to do it, like now, before a big meeting. Josh, her Team Leader, is not at all keen. He is standing in the boardroom doorway, tapping his watch, all cuntish.

Zeynep is twenty-seven and has been working with Erling York's *Financial Risk* team for three years. She uses the word *with* rather than *for* as she is still officially employed by a temp agency, on account of the ongoing volatility of global markets and all that jazz. But she hopes this will change soon. She has been hoping for some time. And she's fine with it. Walahi. Absolutely fine.

Josh has assured her that with continued strong performance, he'll have her put forward for a fixed term contract (*more money, some actual rights*) with the firm by year end. He can do that, he says. It is *within his power (his phrase)*. This presentation to the UPS delegation, he has intimated through a system of nudges, winks and thinly veiled cock-jargon, is the big one. Pun intended. Wink. She puts her mobile phone on mute, scoops up her files and follows him into the refrigerated board room where they are all sat in a circle, wanking. Sorry, waiting. They are definitely just waiting.

After the meeting, Josh is full of how successful it was. He is saying,

"Yes, Zeyns, smashed it! It's in the bag!"

He's offering high fives, which Zeynep only accepts reluctantly, because, urgh, you know, cringe. She is proud of herself, though. She is proud of what she's just done, but Josh's "Go Team!" platitudes don't match with the way she sees what just occurred in there at all.

Josh had done his usual wanker thing. He had delegated almost the entire presentation to her, sitting back in his swivel chair and gazing appreciatively up at her as though she were his protégé or some such shit. Did he even have his feet up at one point? Did she imagine that? Then suddenly, as the meeting seemed to be reaching a natural and utterly uncomplicated conclusion, he had started to bombard her with questions that they had not prepared. What contingencies are there for detecting irregularities in corporate level payment schedules that usually go under the radar of standardised auditing systems? Fuck you, how about that for a contingency?

She knows why he does it. He does it to challenge her. Playing hardball on the client's behalf, showing how they have all the bases covered. This is how he will explain it, later. It is a type of compliment, he has said, in the past.

"It's cos I know you can handle it, Zeyns," he says, always, but she still believes in her heart it is wanker's behaviour.

Trust, fam, she knows loyalty is an old-fashioned concept. She gets that, especially in her line of work. But he is *so extra* sometimes. She can't deny, however, that he is overall an infuriatingly accommodating, generous, even charming sort of boss. So she forgives him for it. Has to. Repeatedly. What choice does she have? This is it. This is her choice.

She walks home. It is a beautiful, balmy, early summer evening in the capital. During the summer she does this every night. It takes her an hour and a half, door to door, from London Bridge to Downs Park Road. She could do it quicker, but she takes the route through Shoreditch then along the short stretch of the Regents Canal, London Fields, and all the way around Downs Park because: wildlife. Walahi, fam, it's mad here. Like Attenborough, or some shit. Right in the city. It was something she hadn't expected. There are no wolves in the United Kingdom (*tragedy*), but sometimes, if she gets up early to walk into work she sees a dirty urban fox (*Vulpes vulpes, so fucking cool they named it twice*). If this happens, she will try to get as close to it as possible, scruffy little *kerata*, before it runs away. She has never touched one. She wonders what that oil flame coat would feel like in her hands. Greasy she bets. But warm. She wonders where they all live.

Her home is (*was?*) Manchester, where her mother and father and her four brothers still live. Before she left, her mother had said this,

"Go, darling, and go now. Do not wait for their permission."

It was the end of a long night at her parents' restaurant and they had sat up late, drinking tea and wine and tea again. They stirred lumps of sugar into the swirling amber of their mint filled *bardagi* and smiled sadly at each other as the dark green leaves waltzed for them, trapped deliriously behind the glass. It was the kind of night that somehow knows it is the end of something, so fills itself with pregnant pauses and images that keep coming back. Zeynep had graduated her MBA a month earlier. Both of them were, in their own ways, restless.

Feeling the need to talk more freely, they had walked hand in hand through the midnight streets, feeling the cool north winds on their oval, olive faces and Zeynep had begun to explain how her degree, well, it was only really useful in the *Big City*. She did not want to run a small business, like her father pretended to do; or enable a man to run one, like her mother had done for years. And besides, they had family there, in London, who would look after her, right? Because she wanted to do proper finance, you know. And she wanted to go somewhere where there were more girls like her, walahi. Her mother stopped her then, silently, with a look that said there was no need to explain any further. It was understood. Mumya. It was always understood before she knew how to say it herself.

***

She avoids work drinks for the rest of the week. She can see that Josh is irritated by this; by her aloofness. But he's excited too. Distressingly so. His pants seem to writhe with an almost prehensile tension. All week he walks around readjusting things, crotchally, every time she knocks back a suggestion or deadpans an all too obvious insinuation. He sometimes looks hurt, moping at her from behind his sandy blond fringe just for a moment, but then he blows it up out of his eyes as if to blow off the moment, laughs casually and directs his attention at some other *eager beaver* (*his phrase, urgh*). This is what the guy is like.

Walahi. For real. Like a child who wants attention. But a child with power and excellent taste in aftershave. A seriously icky combo. She is fairly certain that Josh wants to screw her, which makes her feel… well, it makes her feel all kinds of things, and icky is definitely one of them, but mostly it makes her feel tired.

It is Thursday and she is reading about moorhens. Common moorhens (*Gallinula chloropus*) are native to Northern Europe, but are particularly prevalent in the (*filthy, neglected*) waterways of Southern England. She knows to a certainty there is a well-established nesting spot beneath the canal bridge by Broadway Market. She knows too well. Moorhens are one of the reasons she is avoiding work drinks.

The last time Zeynep got properly drunk, she slept with a moorhen. A family of moorhens, to be exact. It had been a works night out, a Friday, the start of the late Spring Bank Holiday weekend, and they had been caning it in the Fox and Hounds on Kingsland Road, as is the custom. Carly (*Vulvas vulvas*), the one girl on her team that seemed to get Zeynep, she was into animals too, though, you know, only in a sort of *Ooh, yeah, that thing on Netflix* sort of way, had been plying her with shots. Sambuca. Her favourite. Josh was there too, of course. Lurking at the edges. Watching them. There had been some pretty intense moments on previous nights out with Carly: holding hands, long hugs, coming up on the excellent pills Carly always had with her. Josh seemed to have noticed, but this night, Zeynep didn't care. Walahi. She didn't care about a single, wankering thing. She had decided she was going to kiss Carly and that was that. Then: bam! Blackout.

She had woken with the ammonium stench of fresh bird shit singing in her nostrils and the shrill screeching of hungry chicks singeing her ears. Somehow, she had secreted her taut, sinewy frame onto the moss-damp ledge of wall beneath a canal bridge, wrapping herself foetus-wise around the wide, scruffy, bowl-like curvature of a fully populated moorhen's nest. And sponging from the gaps between confusion, twigs and metabolised alcohol came the strangest sense of all: she felt rested. Cosy, even. She had slept well.

Now, anyone who knows the slightest thing about moorhen nesting behaviour will know that they are especially territorial during their brood season (*mid-March to late May*). To encroach on their waterside territory in early summer is the behaviour of a wanton idiot and is a fairly sure-fire way to receive a properly severe pecking. So Zeynep was further surprised to find that – far from being badly beaked-up in the worst possible sense – the adult moorhens were dangling worm offerings before her mud striped face in an act of rank smelling, heart breaking generosity. She couldn't accept, she told them, touched though she was, as she was fighting the fairly immediate urge to be sick into her own mouth. The combination of a gut full of sambuca, fresh fowl shit, and partially regurgitated worm corpse was a novel conundrum and one she felt she could best make sense of alone in a darkened room. So, like an unusually well-mannered troll, she made her excuses, then climbed out ashen faced and algae streaked from the shelter of her bridge lodgings, to skulk gingerly home in the fresh dawn light. As walks of shame go, it was fairly unique.

But not entirely without precedent. Because this was not an isolated incident. No. Whilst she'd been having blackouts for as long as she'd been drinking, what was new was this bedding down with wild beasts. That was a faunal twist that she had not seen coming. But notice had been posted just a few months after her move to London. She had met up with an old uni friend, Elif, south of the river, to get plastered and talk about how the North shat all over London from a human decency perspective and all that jazz.

The night had been going brilliantly. They'd met at Clapham Junction, where Elif immediately reported that she had some banging gear from her guy in Liverpool, so as quick as you could say *toilet cubicle* they were red-nose reminiscing at warp speed, motor-mouthing each other's ears off and properly putting the verbal Doc Martens into the soft-arse South. Then, of course, they started in on the shots. One bewildering, sticky sequence of bars and shot glasses later, Zeynep remembered leaving some club in Brixton, hailing a taxi, then the night after that became a solid, silent slab of black.

What is most concerning in the experience of the accomplished black-out drinker, is not the black hole where memory should be. That is terrifying, in its own way, sure, but it is fairly easy to ignore once you've coped with it a few times. After all, there is nothing at all to look back on, so it is simpler just to look the other way. Go forward, fam, don't linger. What is much scarier than the black-out itself is how quickly it becomes normal. Walahi, fam. It's basic. So long as you came through the night more or less unscathed, and so far, Zeynep always had, black-out nights could keep on happening. Indefinitely. They were judged only by piecing together clues in the days or weeks that followed. Half-typed messages, sent (*shit*) or unsent (*yuss*). The deafening silences or dumb cackling of your assorted friends and enemies. The state of the upholstery that you wake on. The different coloured marks on your flesh. Sometimes, if you were lucky, there would be a lingering, dream-spiked residue that retained the flavour of an evening, bitter or sweet, on the tongue tip of your subconscious, just before you woke.

But the morning after this particular night was as clear and haunting a memory as any Zeynep possessed. Half waking to the scent of turned earth, she'd felt a bristled warmth against her cheek that came to her from the farthest reaches of childhood. She was in her parents´ big bed, playing bears, aged three, with her father. The game of *bears* required him to do little more than to let her crawl beneath his duvet on a Sunday morning and fashion herself a tiny, quilted cave next to his enormous, hairy belly. It had to be a Sunday because it was the only day her father allowed himself to lie in. He had that recent immigrant's work ethic that barely allowed a minute for rest or relaxation. Sundays, then, were precious. As she snorfled and scratched next to the heaving warmth of his expansive gut, he would sometimes pass down teddies and toys. Zeynep would then arrange these about her, before briefing them on how the bad, cold English winter was coming, but they would be safe if they all stayed down there, in their warm cave, hibernating together, until all the bad coldness had gone away. They were safe, she explained, as safe as could be, because the big bear, Baba Balou, would make sure that no one could come in and get them while they slept, and he would keep them all warm too. At this point, she would reach behind her and pat her father on his matted rug of black belly hair, just to show them all, her little pack, how huge and strong the big bear was, and how they really didn't have to worry about anything at all. But as she reached out that morning, beyond the limits of her dreamy recollection, she felt the big bear move and shuffle suddenly, then make a sort of pig-like, snuffling noise that really wasn't part of the game at all. And then she noticed that he didn't feel huge to the touch, but small, and furry, and with lots of moving parts she didn't recognise – and – opening one eye, she found herself not in the imagined parents' bed of her long since past, but very definitely at the opening of a bracken covered badger sett in the middle of what she would later find was Brockley Park, with actual badgers circling around her real head. In reality.

It should have been terrifying. She should have sprung to her feet, screaming, freaked out, carried herself off dutifully to a local sanatorium or loony bin for a thorough psychological going over. I mean, walahi, fam – the state of it! But much like the experience with the moorhens sometime later, Zeynep was not at all afraid. Apart from the rumbling nausea of a slowly brewing hangover, she felt cocooned by a sensation of calm and comfort that seemed to radiate from her animal hosts. She stood, a little coyly, brushed herself off, nodded some respectful goodbyes and then strolled off to find a road sign that would tell her where in shitting-hell-balls she actually was. And that was that. Her secret. Between her and the badgers of, well, Brockley, apparently.

There had been two whole years between those beautiful, beastly shenanigans and she had breathed a word to no one. She had dismissed the first incident as a kind of absurd one off, some battered midnight wander that had ended harmlessly enough, but with the new incident, the bridge thing, she was genuinely troubled. I mean, she'd had to climb in there, pissed, on to a tiny, wet shelf of precarious, nest cradling brickwork. And she'd managed it expertly.

On neither of these prior occasions had she had any premonitory sense that seriously freaky shit (*SFS*) was about to go down, but now Zeynep senses something might be about to happen again. She is about to get her period, which could have something to do with it. Her sixth sense seems to sharpen with the onset of a new menstrual cycle. She can smell bullshit from a hundred yards. Plus, it is nearly pay day, at the start of summer, so there is that buzzy sort of *let's all get completely smashed in a beer garden* tension in the building, too. But the main thing is, Josh is acting up. Like the man-child that he is, he finds it impossible to hide when he is excited about something. When something is up with Josh, it is broadcast in his behaviour. He may bring in cakes or pastries for everyone (*standard*), leave sticky note smileys on your desk (*shrug*) and once, during his own personal push to secure his Team Leader job on a permanent basis, he even installed a series of portable, wireless speakers around the office to play humorous, holiday camp style intercom messages on the hour, every hour, for a whole week. Walahi. Swear down, fam. It was actually quite funny, to be fair. The wanker.

And this Thursday morning, it seems clear to everyone that some announcement is imminent. Every member of the team has arrived at work to find the screensaver messages on their monitors altered to say something excruciatingly cheesy, though nominally motivational. Zeynep's says, "Lone wolf… or leader of the pack?" *(Urgh.)* Carly calls Zeynep over to see her message. It says, "Carly in the Sky with Diamonds." I mean, what the actual fuck? Clearly, thinks Zeynep, Josh is planning something. Something almost always includes bucket-loads of drink, straight after work. So, she does the sensible thing. She keeps her head down and she reads about moorhens. She reads some good long articles about moorhens and then she finishes up early and she goes to head straight home; batten down the hatches. She will not even buy a bottle of wine on the way. No, fam. Safety first. But before she is out of the building, Carly *(Improba nympha)*, calls out to her:

"Watcha, Zeyns! Full moon tonight… be careful out there."

Walahi, fam. Wa. La. Hi.

***

The night passes without incident. Of course it does. I mean, what did she expect? To be transformed into a were-hen, or were-badger or some other fucking kind of were-creature. Come on, fam. Get real. She feels silly but relieved.

In work, that morning, Josh is acting very serious and wearing his name badge, which Zeynep takes to mean someone from *high-up* is in the building. Her suspicions are confirmed later when Carly ushers her over to the coffee machine to spy on Josh, nodding very earnestly, at some bigwig in his office. The bigwig is nodding too and even signing something. So that's it, they decide. Josh is moving on up. Again. His excitability explained. Good for him, thinks Zeynep. He deserves it. The wanker.

Strangely though, Josh still seems somewhat miffed for the rest of the afternoon. He very decidedly does not *bring the bantz* (*yep, his again*) for what remains of the working day, which represents a serious departure from standard practice on a Friday. And this starts Zeynep wondering. Perhaps they have read the whole situation wrong, Carly and her? Perhaps it was bad news Josh was receiving from the bigwig? Those volatile global markets and all that jazz. Her mind starts to race, so to calm herself down, she plugs in her headphones and listens to an audio recording of wolf calls that she has downloaded from the International Wolf Centre at www.wolf.org.

It is working, too. The pained, melodious call of the Eurasian wolf (*Canis lupus lupus*) sings to Zeynep's lonely heart. The recording builds from a series of achingly beautiful single calls ("*there is a love, I reminisce, like a seed I've never sown*"[1]) to the chorusing of a singing pack that rises and falls with the joyous clamour of a harmonious community working in perfect unity. Zeynep closes her eyes to properly enjoy it, when, walahi, fam, for real? Shit! The song is interrupted by that irritating "ping". She opens her eyes and sees a new email in her inbox. It is from Josh and it is one line long: *I know you are listening to those wolves again. My office. Now.*

Zeynep storms into the office without bothering to knock and is already saying,

"Listen, fam, it's late on a Friday, so if this is a piss-take, I'd rather not, you know..."

But Josh's face does not say piss-take. And something in the stern way he is looking up at her stops the rest of the words in her big mouth and she trails off.

"Sit down, Zeyns," he says, gravely.

So, she stops, and she sits, and she looks squarely at him. He is shaking his head slowly, so she readies herself for bad news. She has kind of guessed this moment would come eventually. She has a good idea of what is happening. Temp contracts can be

---

1   Lang Laev – Love and Misadventure

cancelled at a week's notice, so, in truth, she has done well to last this long. She looks in his face, which wears the sullen look of a denied and surly boy, and she sees it. Her mistake is clear. She has been too much herself. She has answered like with like. To Josh's lewd, inappropriate, sometimes funny, sometimes painful cajoling, she has said no, and ha-ha, and fuck you in just the way that his manner has invited. And that is not allowed. That is not how the dynamic is supposed to work.

A man's ego, she has learned this lesson from her Mother, cannot be so honestly handled. A man's self-image, however absurd, must be pandered to, lest you bruise his pride. Bruise his pride and feel his wrath. So, you must tell him the things he needs to hear. Walahi. It is the only way. Yes, it was a good decision, Baba (*hers*). Yes, you have (*she has*) a good head for business, Baba. Yes, Baba, it takes a strong man (*and much stronger woman*) to make something work for this long. They never get past needing that, the men-children who run the world. They will always need the pat on the belly.

"Listen, I'm sorry to have to tell you like this," says Josh, "but… well… "

I'm a coward. You wouldn't let me screw you and that makes me feel weak. I'm uncomfortable with the fact that you are a lesbian. The Turkish are not a trustworthy people. That wolf stuff is just weird. I'm a coward, I'm a coward, I'm a fucking sexist coward.

"…I got you the fucking contract! Three years, baby!"

Well shit, fam. Josh! He came through. The wanker.

***

So, of course there are drinks. Drinks in his office. Drinks in Carly's flat (*woooooh*). Drinks at a champagne bar near Liverpool Street (*on Josh, double woooooooh*). There are lots of drinks, too many drinks, because, well, he has caught her off guard, hasn't he? And he's brought the chang, too, the russell-dust, the good stuff from his top guy, which they do too, together, all three of them, in the toilet of the champagne bar, packed close, pushing up against each other as they dip their heads over fat lines on the grubby white cistern. And then there are more drinks. And more. There are so many drinks and not enough chang to balance them and she is woozy, fam, Woo-Zy. And Josh is always at the edge of things, watching. Arms around them. "My team," he says. Then someone says "Fox". She can't remember if it was him. We've got to go to the Fox, someone says. And, well, doesn't she have a right to celebrate? I mean, walahi, fam – isn't that her right? And Carly looks so good. Soooo fucking good. And this could really be the start of something, of the life she's worked so hard for. And, fuck it, right? Yeah! Fuckitus iticus. So they head to the Fox. And there are even more drinks. Drinks, drnks, dnks in the Fux and Hannnnnds. N of crse, the nite goez black. It gos blck, fm, it go blaaaaaack…

***

The first thing she feels is a vibrating in her tightly clenched jawbone. The tremoring earth rumbles through her skeleton, through her skull, and she is aware that she is lying near a railway track. What she is feeling is the distant movement of an Overground train, communicated through the tremulous movement of the hard earth. Her body feels tired, completely worn out, as though she has run a great many miles and her jaw aches. But her belly feels heavy and full. Not full of alcohol, either, like she expects. Like she knows. It is full of something heavier. Full of meat.

Then come the smells. There is that familiar smell of soil, again, but more: Carly's perfume, blood, piss. She breathes deeply through her nose again to make more sense. The smells tell her everything: the tree bark, moss upon red ochre brick work, fresh carrion, some slightly burnt wholegrain toasty at a local caff, blood congealing on a chewed and splintered name badge, the dew drops in the nettle patch, the blood again, the shit, the railway tracks, cigarette butts, saliva and dried tears… the smells alone tell her exactly where she is. It is strange, but completely normal, too. Standard, fam. Walahi. She is by the railway embankment on the west side of Hackney Downs Park. She knows this. Without opening her eyes, she knows. She is where the foxes live. She is home.

Bear to the Wind: The implausible disappearance of Steven "Bearwind" Deloitte*

A long read by Ged McGreatie

* – Full disclosure, Danny, I'm struggling with the title, pal. There are actually just too many "bear" puns to choose from. I mean, think about it: Bear Faced Cheek – Bearing His Soul – Bear Today, Gone Tomorrow – Going on a Bear Hunt…I mean, take your pick. I'm not arsed and I'm pretty tired, Danny, tbh, pal. I've barely slept. Shit, that's another! I'm just saying, right, I'm not precious here. You said you needed something pronto, so this is it. If you want tae change it, change it. Alright?

Steven "Bearwind" Deloitte should not be a hard man to find. At six foot two and eighteen stone, he cuts a formidable, even imposing, figure in any room. His hulking frame is practically seared into the public imagination: those square, kaftan-clad shoulders, those big paws encrusted with gold. Bear-like, you might say, but don't you dare – because Deloitte was also famed for his unpredictable temper. In the summer of 2018, near the height of his notoriety, he was said to have tossed Price Morgoon* from a luxury yacht into the clear blue waters of Bal Harbour, Florida, just for questioning his choice of deck shoes.

Can we use this? It's denied by Morgoon, the fat prick, but if we say allegedly? Lemme know ASAP.

Hardly a shrinking violet then, and that is before you factor in his profile as one of the leading, if somewhat unorthodox, economic forecasters of the last decade. The self-styled *Investments Shaman* was, until a year or so ago, hosting regular yurt lunches with Dustin Preudhomme in his Laurentian mountain retreat and had been seen holidaying in flagrante in Macrolon's Monaco apartments, his sandy-grey dreadlocks glistening in the d'Azurian sun. Rumour even had it he had been lined up to speak at the World Economic Forum in 2020 on the topic of *Spirit Markets* until Covid hit, draining the resources of the world's economies and with it every last drop of his bulging credibility as the neoliberal elite's go-to guy. You see, Deloitte was the man who tipped the aviation industry to *explode* in 2020, sinking the investment portfolios of a number of notable players in the process. He disappeared without a trace in the April of last year. He has not been seen since. Until, perhaps, just maybe, now…by me*.

Too much? I'm going for the big build up. Yer always banging on about tension, so…

You see, the man I'm surreptitiously eyeballing in this shabby-chic, off-grid cafe on the Rue Amelot, Paris, could easily be Bearwind. I am hot-dogging a tip left by a former associate of Deloitte, one of the few who would speak to me, and it has led me, quite aptly, to the Dreamer Man Café´. I have taken up a seat at the back of the room where, in accordance with the laws of my tribe, I can observe at a safe distance. Just moments ago, a man with a striking resemblance to the mystic-cum-trader took his place by the window and ordered wordlessly with a nod. Comfortable in his environment, it seems he's known here, and if it is him, the big man himself, then he's changed somewhat since his last public appearance. The trademark dreads are gone, but behind the convenient cover of a stylishly hand-stitched, black cloth mask are the same intense, steely eyes, the same rash of silver stubble and the same shade of blond-grey hair that apparently sent Mutti mad with passion, if such a thing can be imagined. The broad shoulders, too, bring to mind the ursine bulk of the man who managed to make bizarre practices such as *speculation sweat lodges*, *biz-chimping* and *soul audits* de-rigueur for much of the last decade. The man for whom Time magazine coined the term "cryptomancy".

But let's stop a moment to consider how we, how he, came to this point. Because the story of Steven Deloitte's rise is as discombobulating (*I know you hate that word, Danny, but it fits, OK, you stuffy prick? It stays in. That's a deal breaker for me*) as his sudden, ghost-like disappearance.

It started, phantasmagorically (*better? All smiles? Yer a snob pal*), more than a decade ago with a teasingly trailed website that appeared somehow attuned to the algorithms of every major social network and search engine in cyberspace. It was the winter of 2009 and any internet inhabitants with a passing interest in, well, anything at all actually, found themselves mystically invited, via banner ads, pop ups and mail-drops simply to *expand*. With a single click on this unassuming, one-word hyperlink, they were transported straight to a landing page and a spectrally glowing passage of text that emerged, impressively, from behind a flash animation of parting clouds. It read:

Namaste, and welcome, to the world of Stephen Bearwind Deloitte: Investments Shaman. Evolve your inner self and revolve *your outer wealth by journeying with us to the convergence of your own hyper-riverised cash flows. From our spiritual vantage point, your financial and Chakric horizons will look a whole lot wider. When you combine ancient Buddhist teachings, Native American wisdom and the shamanic practices of the Amazonian Wood Elders, the result is a powerful financial management tool like none offered in the conventional field of market trading. Take my hand/access the links below to begin expanding your mind and financial assets… exponentially*.*

* I took this verbatim from www.bearwinddeloitte.org, but the page has since been taken down. As recently as last week, actually. I couldnae get a screen shot. Soz about that, pal. I know it makes us look less credible. You can try and poke around yerself if you want, but really, what's the point? I mean, we've been flogging this for a year, Danny. Through a fucking plague, while half the world burns. Let's just get this out now, aye?

Wood elders? Chakric horizons? Hyper-bloody-riverised? For many who visited – and there's a good chance you were one of them, because the numbers here are staggering (the hit rate of the page was in the big-auld-millions within its first week of going live), the site itself seemed like a joke; the frothy mind-gush of a hit and run wrong-bonce. But it is a very human trait to read poignancy in pish; holiness in horseshit. It was not long before Deloitte was posting swinging-dick-pic-testimonials of *very* satisfied investors, all attesting to his otherworldly market forecasting prowess. The mystique around him grew… exponentially.

How did he do it? Were the fixers in? The 'illuminati wearing friendship bracelets' was how some critics described Bearwind's unlikely success. A cursory rummage through the man's pre-fame past throws up some hints as to what was to come. Before the Bearwind incarnation, Deloitte was exploiting the trading boom of the late eighties, by offering surprisingly popular *biz-chimping* workshops. These highly secretive, deeply unorthodox brainstorming* sessions often resulted in the exchange of more than ideas, with human shit being flung, allegedly, along with fat wads of cash – hinting strongly at the now well documented developments that were to follow. Deloitte was making a name for himself – or rather –capitalising on the one he already had. Born Steven Erland Deloitte in Caster St. Edmunds, 1972, to a family of fairly unspectacular bankers, the moniker alone held connotations of big league, which many naturally assumed equalled links to the shady, super-rarefied world of elite investment. The Bearwind appendage seemed only to manifest somewhat later, with the appearance of the website.

Is that allowed now? Does it piss off epileptics, or something? Or is everyone over that? I can't keep up. Lemme know, okay?

So…what was that the secret? Friends in high places? Well, if we listen to the man himself, that might not be too far from the truth. Only, we may need to set our sights that little bit higher than the super-rich suspects that most would have in mind, to somewhere beyond the stars. Take this, from an interview with Forbes in 2012:

By communing with the spirit world in a climate of cross-dimensional growth synergy, I can unlock secrets usually reserved for celestial clients. The spirits are as interested in expanding wealth horizons as we are. You've just got to possess the paranaturalised comms tools to interface with them.

Well, of course. Paranaturalised communcation – what could be more…natural? The tools, it seems, to which Bearwind was most inured included a bewildering smorgasbord of psychoactive potions and powders, all of which featured DMT compounds (the spirit molecule, as it is widely billed) as their key ingredient. Interested parties paid exorbitant fees for a consultation, in which Bearwind would accompany a delegation of representatives to his Bolivian jungle resort, before stripping them of their clothes and performing a *shamanic flame descaling* that required participants to burn their ties. Naked, pale and quivering – the "Kelvins" – a temporary, stock name issued after the stripping away of earth titles, participants in the early days were invariably men, though, later, accommodation was made for a number of "Karens" -would be led into a morass, where they would daub each other with bat faeces and natural dyes, before lying face down on a linen sheet, to undergo *a transactional baptism*, a process which assigned them a spirit animal for the duration of their stay. These transcendent identities were garnered by matching the stained imprint left on the befouled linen after each exalted face plant to the corresponding silhouetted *business beast* on a pre-prepared chart.

The final, spirit-mangling act saw the introduction of a trolley-based panoply of mind-altering substances, which were placed at the centre of a ring of consecrated whiteboards and multi-coloured marker pens. Delegates would then be invited to let their "business beast" run wild. Falling on the cache like superannuated meth-heads – accountants were known to be unusually ravenous – the proto-tribe would gorge themselves sacred for as long as an hour, before setting about the boards, all tweaked and inky. At the end of the twenty-four to thirty-six hour *meeting*, the whiteboards, Deloitte's website has claimed, were almost always populated with complex financial forecasts, business models and/ or algorithms that could be used to immediately penetrate emerging global markets or competently manage three to five-year corporate planning cycles. The delegates themselves were usually bereft afterward, broken and weeping, sleeping in recovery hammocks for a day or more. But the reviews spoke for themselves. Participants reported emerging from the forest with a new-found, New Age sensibility, a deep-seated respect for the mystery of the cosmos and pretty enormous EBIT figures to take back to head office*.

Talk about getting trollied, right? I can try to work that in if you like? No, sorry, that's shite. Christ, I'm tired. And I know that you wanted more dirt here...something on the Swedish guy who returned to Stockholm "with tits", but I couldn't track down your source. IKEA just aren't talking, pal. You're going to have to cut me some slack on that one. Or maybe just don't print this shite, right? I mean, it's fucking dross, right? What is it with you and this guy? It feels like a vendetta, pal, I'll be honest. What happened to the stuff I sent you on those union busting cunts? Not sexy enough, aye? I don't know, Danny. It's a fucking shame, pal.

For a while, this reputation for chemically enhanced practices meant the big brutes of global finance, those with triple 'A' reputations to maintain, kept their distance. But it was also a time when the painfully slow recovery from recession meant anyone turning any sort of profit gained traction pronto. Whatever his methods, spiritual or shady, Deloitte's popularity and portfolio steadily grew. Spotting a hole in otherwise ice clad markets through which to reel in the trophy fish he craved, Bearwind quickly moved to diversify his range of forecasting tools to include an arsenal of *entirely natural, bio-organic, conscience reframing options*. What, then, were his most popular services? This list, again taken from the now defunct website, gives a disturbing flavour:

- *Ayahuasca Analytics Camp*
- *Bogota Bumper Package (team bonding)*
- *Cancun Hospitality Package (elite clients only)*
- *Geist Enhanced Steam-bath and Blue Sky Session-growth focus*
- *Geist Enhanced Steam-bath and Blue Sky Session - streamlining focus*

- *Future Markets Maturation Pod (vegan)*
- *Future Markets Maturation Pod (with toad)*
- *Psychoactive Forecast and Modelling (standard)*
- *Psychoactive Forecast and Modelling (bungee)*
- *Soul Audit*
- *Speculation Sweat Lodge*
- *Yurt Consultation with Peyote spiked crudités*
- *Yurt Lunch (elite clients only)*
- *Wood Elders Full Retreat (elite clients only, subject to Wood Elder availability)*

And though the list may read like a corporate love-in curated by Coldplay, it also happens to contain just as many hits. So successful were these assorted services, that celebrity endorsement – and soon, status – were quick to follow. Sally Haymek spoke in glowing terms of the 2014 *Soul Audit* she received before investing in a string of Hollywood hits as an executive producer. Neil Patrick Harris practically set up residence in Bearwind's Utah ranch, which may go some way to explaining his enduring appeal. But it was when, in the April of 2018, Deloitte was seen breakfasting with Geoff Bezios[2] at the 2018 Bush Centre Forum for Leadership, that the Bearwind brand exploded.

Suddenly, anyone who was anyone wanted the wind in their faces. And, if at all possible, they wanted it blasted through a tuba; Bearwind's *Orchestral Coloninquiries* were an alleged under the table offer, reserved exclusively for private clients. Bonio, typically, led the charge. He moved quickly to set up a bi-weekly, online *intention trammelling* three-way between Bearwind, himself and a renowned Peruvian herbalist known only as Little Salty. The sessions were designed ostensibly to guide the financial direction of Bonio's continued charity work, though a subsequently filed super-injunction prevents us from

2 "Breakfast with Bezios: the Bearwind Blows into Town." Ged McGreatie, The Telegraff, April 20th, 2018.

saying any more. Finance ministers, economic analysts, Fortune 500 stat sniffers – everyone jumped in line. By September 2019 Steven Bearwind Deloitte's estimated worth stood at \$280 billion. The *Year of the Bear* ended with a banquet in Beijing as the private guest of Xii Pimping. It still isn't clear what exactly was on the menu*.

* Listen, Danny, I've looked into this and that's as far as I'm prepared to go. Christ, an allegation like that could ruin us both, pal. Let's just leave the thing hanging, yeah, if you'll pardon the pun.

There were controversies too, of course. When Randy Juiliano briefly visited Bearwind's Cancun resort in 2016, he followed it immediately with a fortnight in a private clinic suffering from catastrophic rectal discharge. A later lawsuit contesting the contents of one of the Bearwind brand's *spirit flushing shakes*, found that ingredients that had been listed as "solar ionised, repurposed marsh waters of historic, tribal settlements" had in fact been the sun warmed ditch piss of a nearby building site. The case was settled out of court.

And Bearwind's personal transgressions raised some eyebrows too. The alleyway battery of a hot yoga instructor was never pinned to the big man's rap sheet, but when the actual sheets of a Swiss hotel ended up soggy at the 2018 meeting of the Bilderberg group, a number of notorious right-wing bedwetters insisted that Bearwind foot the bill. After a period of on/off relationships that same year, in which he was reported to have dated both the Minogue sisters, the pair were unanimous in their appraisal of Bearwind as a *wet-leg*. This corresponds with at least one of my sources who, though he sadly declines to be named, referred to Deloitte more than once as "an absolute bell".*

* You want even more here, Danny? You keep mentioning dirt. I heard something about Gwyneth Paltrow and a malfunctioning

aqua-pod. 200 gallons of whale pish, or something? It's not corroborated, but people will believe anything after the minge candle. But if you want me to dig up more, you'll have to push back that deadline, pal. I'm on ma arse, here, tbh. Shelley's talking about leaving us, again. Taking the kids, you know. Says she's losing respect for me. Shite, can you blame her? I'm barely ever home. So I'd really rather not go through the bins again, this time, you know? Metaphorically or otherwise.

So how to square all that with the man sat before me on this flaccid Friday in Paris? Big and daddish with a whiff of washed-up surf dude, he looks somewhat uneasy in his cream coloured, crumpled cheesecloth shirt. He chomps intently on French galette instead of scouring the horoscopes or business sections. Can this really be the man who wowed the heady world of international finance? I study him more closely a wee while. The afternoon light through the floor to ceiling windows is kind on those creased but handsome features. His wiry silver hair is close cropped right down to the eyebrows, under which dart those famously deep set, steel blue eyes. He holds a fountain pen in his right hand which he nervously chews or taps on the table at intervals. His right leg is bobbing anxiously too; tell-tale signs of stress. Occasionally, he jots down a note or two in his Moleskin notebook, but he seems too distracted to follow any thought for long. This is a man who is troubled, hunted, but despite this, I feel sure that, so far, at least, he has not noticed my attentions. Around him, patrons move and cups clink insouciantly against saucers. The waiter refreshes his pot with hot water and the steam drifts dreamily in the pale sunlight. MacBooks open and close like clapperboard scene markers. This is a place that a certain kind of person could find peace, though for a hack like me, it is pure theatre. I am ever more engrossed, when suddenly, I notice that Bearwind's gaze is taken by a scene in the street outside. Out there, across the boulevard, a young, androgynous

Parisienne with green hair struggles to unlock a hire-scooter with a smartphone app. She looks back in our direction and shrugs. Bearwind smiles. I smile with him. Eating, he lifts his mask to one side momentarily, to pop in a crumbling chunk of pastry or sip at his Lapsang, before hooking it back over his ear fastidiously. Is that a gold tooth I spot, as he takes a bite? The man was known for them. But it's too late. He's masked again. And despite the lingering smile, there is a sadness in his eyes*.

You know, I used to think this would be glamorous. I was bang into it. Hotel in Paris? On the scent of a story? Big game in ma sights. But I don't know, pal, it all just feels a bit shabby, these days, you know? I mean who is this Bearwind cunt, at the end of the day? Only what we make him, right? Following these pricks round, writing stories, building their mystique. I mean, they're the fucking worst, sure – posh cunts who'd sooner have their own planet than mix wi' the rest of us. But what does that make us, Danny, eh? Following them? Worshipping them? Sniffing their artisan upholstered bike seats? I'm having a moment, pal, tell the truth. I'm not sure this is for me anymore. You can have this copy here, then I'm off home. Have a proper talk with Shelley. Get some things straight. And this hotel is shite, by the way.

It's a look that has me wondering… how easy is it to disappear? For most of us, I'm sure it's nothing. A midnight flit and reliable mode of transport ought to do it. Put a bit of distance between yourself and the folks who know you, ditch the old accounts, get a new name and phone contract: job done. But for a titan like Bearwind? Where do giants hide, exactly? And how long can they stay hidden? Once you've taken the alpine air at Davos, can you ever go back to sucking back on the toxic street guff that the rest of us mortals live on? Isn't it natural for a shyster, particularly a good one, just to reinvent the trick and try again? It seems to be the way of things these days, doesn't it? Hide in plain sight. Award yourself a bonus. Brazen it out. Couldn't Bearwind, buffeted by at least some of his billions, have done the same? On this point though, at least, Deloitte's motivations are understandable. There are people, important people, who want him, if not dead, then certainly pretty badly harmed. Even former secretaries, people who worked closely with the slush-fund Sauron through his most profitable years, now deny his existence. As a journo, I've grown accustomed to hearing that fabled phrase *no comment* on a fairly regular loop, but the omerta-hush over this story has been something else altogether. It really is as though he never was. And if just knowing the man is so risky, I ask myself, do I really want to be the one to blow his cover? *

Is that what's going on here, Danny? You want to flush the guy out, right? You were in with this guy, weren't ye? Lost some money, did ye? Is it revenge ye want, pal? Well, I'm nae doing it, alright. This is as much as you're getting. I've had enough. It's all so bloody tawdry. So bloody pointless. I'm arf ta learn crochet, or baking, or some shit. Something wholesome, you know. Making fucking flans has got tae be better than this shite. Get someone else to do yer grubbing, pal. This is it for me. What is it those dragon cunts say? Aye – that's it – I'm oot.

But in the end, aren't we all just creatures of habit? Our behaviours repeat, the same patterns emerge. We go back to what we know, even if it kills us, in the end. And studying his movements, the way he fiddles with his cup, tips it gently toward the table, I see he has poured some tea leaves from the pot onto the porcelain plate and is pushing them around, pensively. This is no idle teasing. There is method in this meddling. And then it dawns on me… he's reading the signs. He's seeing banknotes in the backwash, making a tasseographic plan. This saucer-based sorcery is the last sign I need. And now it is I who can't resist following my instincts. My habitual defaults kick in, my snidey-senses tingling. Almost on auto pilot, I slink up next to the empty chair behind him, keeping a respectful, virus-fearing distance. I clear my throat and say:

"So, Steven. What do you see? Any tips you can give me?"

For a moment he does not move, does not so much as tilt his head, but in his stillness is the frozen brace of something trapped. He snorts a sort of half laugh. He pushes out his chair and presses down his shirt, flattening it against that wide chest with those big palms. He is pretending he hasn't understood the question. But I know how close I am now. The old tracker's instincts push me on.

"It's Steven Bearwind Deloitte, right? Investments Shaman?"

He stands then turns my way and looks down at me. If his intention is to intimidate, then it one-hundred-percent works. I start to feel all knock kneed; like Merkel, but without that sturdy, German frame. I've broken cover. I feel exposed, silly and I want to run away. The man is giant and there is a glint of wickedness in his eye, too.

"Get the galette, kid," he says, smiling from underneath the mask and winking at me, before turning on his heels and adding, over his shoulder, "it's very good."

Trembling and thrilled, I have the instinct to follow him, pin him to a fixed abode, seal the deal. It's only natural; part of the job. Hack journalism 101: get an address. Always get an address. But I resist. Something in the calm way he departs, the ease with which he leaves, the way he lets the door swing softly closed behind him as he nods to the waiter; it all suggests to me that he'll be back. He´s left a fifty euro note on his table. A calling card, perhaps, I have the instinct to collect it, harvest it for clues. But like a wizened highland tracker at the end of a long trail, it feels somehow enough just to have glimpsed this rare beastie up close, without the need to shoot him through the heart. Instead, I watch as he hops awkwardly onto a scooter himself, wobbles a little, then simply glides away, all one-hundred-or-more kilos. I stay and take his advice. My first piece of shamanic trammelling from a man who once had the ear of every major financier in the developed world. I get the galette and it tells me everything I need to know. It has to be Bearwind. Because it tastes like shit.

This article was never published by Vize Corp Publishing because of the threat of legal action from the representatives of Mr. Deloitte. The reprinting here of this unedited draft is against the express wishes of Mr. Deloitte and, according to him, the Wood Elders of several, unknowable denominations.

Ged McGreatie, owner of McGreatie's Scottish Galette PLC, is no longer associated with Vize Magazine and has received no financial benefit from the reprinting of this draft piece, which was obtained without his knowledge. (Probably from his bin.)

To Be the Cat

Chamomile tea with a little honey. To clear her head, chamomile tea with a little honey was what she should definitely drink now. She, Anna, did not know where the idea had suddenly come from. She, Anna, was a habitual coffee drinker, but she felt now instinctively that this would be the thing to calm her down and lend some clarity to the situation. Maybe it was his dickhead name? Chamomile. Calm-o-miles. Whatever. It was perfect. She would go somewhere and have it.

Miles, Anna's long-term partner, was the dickhead who had just talked her mobile phone hot. Not warm. Hot. His long, lachrymose whining testing the attritional capacity of even the almighty Samsung corporation's latest device. She felt its buzz of radiation baking her hand and seeping through her jacket pocket as she wondered vaguely about the damage such things did over time. She felt a tension headache strap on and tighten up along a familiar tract between her temples. She was resisting taking too much 'pain relief' during the day. So, with a very specific tonic in mind, she left the house headed to a cafe near the dock road, one she knew, though not all that well, and took a seat by the bay window to look out over the grey expanse of the familiar pebble beach. She ordered the drink and, as she waited for it to arrive, she removed a writing pad from her cloth bag and placed it in front of her.

She looked down at the empty page. She wrote out the title of the current problem: Spanish Whore and underlined it. She wrote the date, too, 10th November 2018. She intended to think this through logically.

Anna was a woman betrayed. That was the category into which she had fallen. Miles, the betrayer, had fucked a Spaniard on a late summer business trip, and though this had occurred more than two months ago, their relationship, a marriage of eight years in all but documentation, had ceased to function ever since.

Not that the relationship had been functioning well prior to 'the whore', as Miles was at pains to point out. He hauled out the same lines every time the topic was returned to. They related to her 'emotional coldness' or some such nonsense, and the topic was all they returned to, every evening of every day and for whole days on weekends, even after he had succumbed to Anna's insistence that he move out of the house and into a rented apartment for an unspecified 'short while'. They had griped and squabbled intermittently before 'the whore', mostly about work or politics. They'd had irregular, if sometimes successful, sex. But now, even that sorry state of affairs whispered from memory like an unattainably paradisiacal hinterland. And that, clearly, was his whore loving fault.

The situation was untenable. The easiest thing to do would be to leave him, but Anna burned with an indignant resistance to such a collapse. She still wanted Miles, or at least, she thought she did. She wanted him to want her, she knew that much. But no matter how much she gandhied herself against the allure of vengeance, she felt strongly that he needed to be punished, and punished by her, before they could ever move forward again. She brushed her dark brown hair from her pale face and pressed the tip of her ballpoint pen into the page, hard.

She revisited her options. She had conceived more than once of something that included pushing oranges into his mouth – huge, swollen, Valencian oranges. The oranges, sticky and fleshy in her mind, represented the fulsome tits of the undoubtedly buxom Spanish whore he'd fucked. She did not know if 'the whore' was in reality buxom, Miles would not confirm any details about her, but she knew to a certainty that Miles was a tit man. She saw the way his eyes moved at parties. She had viewed his internet search history. So, it seemed quite apt to her that he should gorge on them, these orange-tits, these unctuous orbs; be force fed them by her, titless Anna, stuffing him with orangey tit-mass until the tit-pulp oozed through his nostrils and tit-juice spilled from his eyes like luminous, fragrant tears.

Or she could cut his dick off. But then that would be the end of it and awfully messy. Plus, a sizeable part of the appeal of keeping him would be lost anyway. Miles had a more than serviceable dick, though she was careful not to mention this too often in his presence, for the fear of him becoming yet more cockproud. This pride of his also kept her from pushing through with one of her original ideas, that he should make some sort of public admission of guilt on social media, reading a statement prepared by her to camera. She knew he would find this humiliating, but also suspected a part of him would be pleased that his promiscuity with Spanish whores should pass into public knowledge, and she was not prepared to cede him this satisfaction.

As Anna pondered these assorted malices, warmed by them and the sweet aroma of chamomile and honey lifting from her cup, she realised that she had been sketching a picture upon her notepad for some time. It was the picture of a cat. And not just any cat. Her cat. Her first. Her only. It was a picture of Spock. All black but for one white splodge just above his nose and the prim albino boots he wore on every foot, Spock possessed a place in Anna's psyche unmatched by any other person, creature or thing. He was there in her earliest memories and had been with her for the full span of her childhood – toddlering, tinkering and teenaging at her side until the long overdue, but still untimely, expiry of his ninth life, just weeks after her own sixteenth birthday.

Anna remembered how her parents had worried that his death might derail her preparation for the GCSE exams, but they needn't have. Anna learned then and learned well that the best way to use grief, anger – anything painful and heavy and hot – was to force it down deep and smelt it into a white fury that could be channelled and moulded to her will. She shut herself in her room and studied like a fanatic. She sobbed in bursts, forcing out tears in flurries of angry coughs before pawing her red eyes dry, then hacking through another solid hour of quadratic equations. She stayed up late. She barely ate. The colour around her dark eyes bruised with a deep purple that remained proudly to this day. And when the results came, it had clearly all been worth it. She attained ten A*s and one A. But she never spoke his name to anyone again.

Spock, so called not, as most assumed, for his ears, which pointed pertly above his tiny little kitten head like punkish ornament, but for her own two-year-old inability to say his original name correctly. Spot became Spock in Anna's infant mouth – and as he was so undeniably her pet, her parents having little time for distractions, that, by dint of repetition, it stuck.

Anna had no brothers or sisters, but Spock had been a sibling and more. He'd followed her everywhere. Her favourite memory of him, of them, had taken place on the beach just yards from this cafe, out on *The Cob* – the seafront where people took their pets for walks. Yes, those pets were ordinarily dogs, but Anna knew of no rules, no signs or stipulations, that precluded cats from walking there too.

At six years old, Anna had already developed the parentally terrifying predilection of wandering off on her own whenever the desire took her. Her parents were so often busy that she reprised this trick many times. Living so close to the beach, she sometimes left the house at random and went to throw pebbles on the stony Cob which stretched out into the Atlantic just sixty yards from the door of her family home. On this particular occasion she had decided to take Spock with her.

And why not? Why shouldn't he go with her? He was her pet just as those dogs belonged to those other people that tramped daily up and down wearing their big stupid boots, chunky knits and goofy smiles. Yes, he should come along, no question, but properly. She had noticed that most of those doggies had leads. At least until they got across the road and onto the further stretches of the stony shore, they were kept on leads. Anna found a ball of green twine in the hallway drawer, unravelled a length and hacked it free with a carving knife which she had taken from the perennially unattended dishwasher. She then tied it roughly around the velveteen collar of her obedient and dutiful cat, sat back and looked at him proudly. He was ready. Wearing only her pyjamas, she pulled on her yellow leather boots and slipped quietly from the front door, tugging Spock behind her.

Though reluctant at first, bleary-eyed and staggering like some drunk hauled unexpectedly from his favourite dive, the cat hit his stride within a few metres. Anna marched proudly ahead and Spock nimbly trotted – her tiny prancing dressage horse, his little white boots seemingly fashioned for just such an occasion – both enjoying the display. They crossed at the lights, again, quite properly, where they first started to attract some puzzled looks and double takes. They made it across the road safely and on to the beach itself, before the experience started to sour.

It was the cold end of a wet autumn and taking one step onto the chill, unfamiliar surface of the stony beach sent Spock darting up onto Anna's left shoulder for safety, where he dug his claws into her skin and clung for dear life. He would not be removed by force nor cunning. He would not do her bidding, which was to strut around the beach confidently like all those silly doggies, chase Anna into the spray of a cresting wave like something off a toilet roll advert, just generally enjoy it. Instead, he sat there, trembling, a real scaredy-cat. When Anna threw a stick for him to chase, he simply looked at her with a confused indifference.

Anna started to brood. A fat, icy rain drop landed, splot, in the centre of her crown along with the knowledge that her father would soon be about them, chasing and scolding. A grim mood rolled over her as the clouds darkened above. She remembered the feeling of the cat – her cat – as the rain really began to pour; bedraggled and drenched, desperately shivering against her neck. She felt no pity for him then. He had disobeyed her at her most wilful. He was a traitor. All was lost. She stared out at the sea and felt its icy numbness.

It was only later, when her parents retold the story to their wine-supping, middle class cronies as something quite other than an anecdote about parental neglect that she felt proud of them both. She was proud of them for refusing to *be good*. For not doing as they were told. Even as they'd heard the shouts of her angry father over the distant tolling of the Sunday bells and the rain streaked through her thin cotton pyjamas, they had both refused to budge. And as she smiled to herself at this thought, she found that she was no longer in the cafe at all. She was back there, in the same spot, standing at the hard edge of the surf, refusing to look back, gazing out upon a wild, black sea – soaked to the skin.

The water warmed, swirled around her, bore her up. Anna closed her eyes and let herself sway backwards. Her head plunged beneath the steaming lip of the bath, under the hot water and she held herself there, her arms pinned to the enamel, staring up through the suds, listening for that delicious dull clanging of pipes, letting the cloudy water sting her eyes. When she finally resurfaced, she was holding a warm sponge to her foo and considering masturbation. She started to press on the sponge in pulses so that it rubbed rhythmically against the hood of her clit and she moaned a little, but, even as an enjoyable warmth started to spread outward, a new image was forming in her mind. It was the image of George Galloway.

Few people want George Galloway in their bathtub and Anna did not want him there then. He was ruining the moment. She did not want to masturbate with or to George Galloway. She tried to push him out and push the sponge down harder into her labia minora, humming to herself to focus her concentration, but it was no good; he was there, squatting in her water and smoothing his creamy white whiskers with a repulsively licked wrist.

Anna huffed and splashed the sponge down dejectedly into the water. The scent of the chamomile bath salts she had bought on her soggy walk home rose about her and she rested her head on the slope of the bath, then closed her eyes. "Okay then," she thought. What was it that George wanted to say to her? Why was he here? She replayed the infamous scene from the reality TV series that everyone was familiar with.

"Do you want me... to be the cat?" asked not-so-gorgeous George, his syrupy, Scottish drawl dripping an all too obvious lust into the palm of his Scandinavian keeper. She blushed, she literally blushed, with embarrassment for the man – a known and implausibly still-active politician – who was damned to degrade himself in the living minds of millions, over and over, for as long as memory or telecommunications lasted with an act of physical theatre so desperately un-erotic that it possessed the power, twelve years later, to stop a wank in its tracks.

She submerged herself again and screamed into the soapy water. It was only later, meticulously padding down the lumps in her duvet before climbing into her pristine, king size bed, the same bed her parents had once slept in, that she understood the relevance of Mr. Galloway's watery remonstrations. George was Miles. Or could be. Should be. Galloway was a living demonstration of the way that a lustful, even proud man, could be forced, or at least cajoled, to prostrate himself before the jurisdiction of a dominant, female demagogue. To be made, by her own hand... just how did Miles always put it? Ah yes, that was it: To be made a cunt of.

***

Miles was pathetically easy to convince. Disappointingly so. All the way down the motorway to Cardiff and then all the way back she itched with an angry dissatisfaction. First, because of Miles's submission: "Sure darling. Yes, of course, darling...I mean, it could even be fun, couldn't it?" Urgh. Then with the way his invasive feebleness had so distracted her and almost ruined her performance, hers, Anna's, of a specially commissioned solo entitled *A Song For All Of Europe* with more bizarre and unwanted pseudo-sexual imagery.

This is how it had happened. Anna Linsky was a soprano of some repute and had been steadily building that reputation in Britain and beyond when she'd met Miles, an Account Development Representative for the British wing of a small but international German tech firm. They had met after one of her shows. They had, it seemed, some mutual friends – so Miles used his 'connections' to pop up in different parts of the country, effectively stalking her on her first real nationwide tour, with that stupid, immediately suggestive grin she'd later come to hate on his face, black fringe flopping foppishly in front of his eyes and always holding two glasses of champagne to toast her 'brilliance'. She had been flattered; she could not deny that. She asked him more than once how he could justify such enthusiasm and financial outlay for a relatively minor performance he'd seen multiple times, but he just made some pun on his name about 'going the extra Miles', then laughed, too loudly, every time, at his own joke.

Anna, dark, slender and beautiful with a talent that seemed to belong to a different age, was the type of woman that a certain class of man felt irresistibly drawn to owning in some way. Although in principle Anna found the sentiment objectionable, Miles's dominant posturing and near obsessive insistence that they would 'make a great team' had been attractive to her. She liked to be wanted. It still felt like something novel back then, not long out of uni where she'd studied Music Composition and was still uncertain of her own elite status. He became her lover and then her manager after convincing her that 'contacts, contracts, all that shit' were his speciality. It was an arrangement that worked for a while, until the scale of Anna's success started to leave Miles overreached. For all his upper-middle-class confidence and sub-Etonian networking, he simply didn't have the language skills or business acumen to broker the international tours and recording deals that Anna's success inevitably led to. He was quietly, but diplomatically, side-lined.

It was then that they started to bicker about politics. Miles believed in Conservative values largely because that's what his father taught him to do and, from a young age, he had come to see his father, despite his many, many transgressions, as an infallible model of manhood and source of all proper opinions. Anna, the daughter of two distant but in their own way principled music teachers, had always voted Labour. Her father was a second-generation Polish immigrant with romantic notions of international brotherhood, whilst her mother was the daughter of dour Scottish Quakers. This interesting heritage had made for fairly interminable dinner table discussions, which had not quite succeeded in putting Anna off politics entirely. Both her parents had died within six months of each other, a year after her meeting Miles, when she was just twenty-five. A heart attack took him, her father, in February before breast cancer killed her mother later that same year. Miles had been stunned by her ability to process it. He'd been awed by her; he'd said so. She barely missed an engagement. Worked harder, if anything. She told him she couldn't afford to stop, and later, he acknowledged it was a time that had been pivotal in her ascent to the top of the British operatic scene, such as it was.

She could never tell anyone that she hadn't found it all that hard. Her lack of grief for her parents was the private shame she carried with her everywhere. Her loyalty to their political values felt like a gesture towards the bond they *should* have had. She had inherited their house and took their quaint, immigrant beliefs as part of the deal.

When they'd met, Miles had needled Anna playfully with his stuffy concept of real world politics and dismissal of her daft, egalitarian Romanticism. It had been a form of flirtation, really: the big man with the hard-headed politics. It had continued like this for a few years, something light and faintly humorous. Miles respected her loyalties, and, after all, politics didn't really affect their lives on a day-to-day level, however much they liked to debate it. But it was when Miles had taken up the mantle of British independence from Europe that he really began to get her goat. Here was an issue that would impact them, their freedoms, their right to live and work where they wanted, directly. Anna still harboured dreams of moving to Italy, dreams that Miles had encouraged, even shared. Then Anna installed Violetta as her European manager and promoter, leaving Miles a kind of honorary role as her domestic agent, and he underwent a change of heart.

He was suddenly, decidedly anti-Europe. He would return home from golfing weekends in Buckinghamshire with his father spouting rubbish about restrictive European legislation or the dangers of open borders. He would hold court whenever possible on how the German techno-crats had bullied the poor Greeks – as if he gave a hoot about Greek factory workers, and were becoming the de-facto central managers of the apparently poisonous *Eurozone*. She reminded him that they both worked in international fields. What kind of person seriously argued for such a nakedly idiotic, self-sabotaging policy? Even taken from a right-wing economic perspective it was moronic. She called him Nigel and ridiculed him even, or rather especially, in front of their friends. It was funny, for a while.

Then, of course, it happened. The idiots actually won. Anna noticed immediately how Miles's anti-European arguments had lost their bite. He no longer seemed convinced that liberation from the bureaucrats of Brussels would result in a new golden age of Beautifully-British-Britishness ™. He worried openly about the economic impact on the continent and, now that he worked for an affiliate company of the Deutsche Bahn, how his own job prospects might be affected. Anna realised, to her great distaste, how little Miles had believed in the things he had argued for. She watched as his once irritating, but undeniably macho, bullishness receded into something altogether more sheep like. And she teased him with this too. Taunted him relentlessly. Taunted him, unfairly, as her own star continued to rise and, due to her much vaunted public support for the Remain campaign, she became the national poster girl and go-to TV guest for a soaring, operatic, unity-loving vision of pro-European togetherness. And then, the whore.

The whore, clearly, had been Mile's last stab at asserting his masculine sense of primacy in their somewhat struggling relationship. And what symbolism he'd imbued it with, she had to grant him that. Her, touring the country, the gallant remoaner, singing her heart out for a borderless Europe as he -the once-proud Brexiteer -so flagrantly exploited the Schengen agreement to sow his decidedly mealy English oats on foreign soil. It was a bold move, bating her with her own flag, but what followed was so obsequious as to make her sick. He *told* her. He confessed.

He'd kept his Spanish shame a secret for less than a week on returning from his trip, a week in which he'd acted so shiftily that she'd known something was sure to come out. The bronze of his Valencian tan had barely begun to fade when, at her mention of tapas over Friday night wine, he had spilled all. The whore, he wept, had been his cry for help. She'd meant nothing, of course. He loved her, Anna, more than ever and he knew that now. Knew how lucky he was. Felt if they could only start to talk, they could be better, he could be better. He was willing to do anything, just name it, anything. It was so unlike the man she'd known, it was pathetic. So pathetic, that she almost missed ´Nigel´.

And so by this confluence of events, did she, Anna Linsky, come to be standing on a Cardiff stage in front of ten thousand opera enthusiasts, imagining getting off with Nigel Farage. It was the line about "Looking to your side to see, A continent of friends; of Unity!", but as she opened her arms wide to unlock her diaphragm and unleash the crowning glory of that high C, the words caught in her throat, and all she saw in the blinding of flood-lights was the open mouth of the UKIP leader, his thick, lying tongue searching out her own, tangling with it, dancing with it, warping her voice, choking the song at its source with its turgid investigation. She clipped the note short, affecting a deliberate staccato emphasis, and gave a little embarrassed cough. The crowd erupted. She exited the stage to rapturous applause, sweating profusely. She had gotten away with it, this time. But the oily taste of gammon swam unctuously in her mouth and she knew one thing. She would call Miles the moment she got home and bring the performance, whatever it was, forward. The sooner she could get all of this done with, the better.

***

She dressed the house, or the four renovated rooms of it that she now lived in alone, with the soft light of candles. She swallowed some Zopiclone and sipped on a large glass of red wine, which she kept almost full at all times. The house was cool and still. Her tenants above and below were not at home, which came as a relief. The soothing sound of the ocean drifted on the breeze through the thumb length gaps she liked to keep in the sash windows, gently rippling the crushed linen curtains. The day passed in bubbles, opaque little pockets of time that seemed to float and burst remotely, untethered, as though she were not directly involved, but merely watching her own life back from some safer chamber, far removed. Whenever she sat down and closed her eyes, she felt the world topple slowly backwards and the sound of the ocean rush between her ears, so she busied herself checking on the flickering flames of the tea lights, arranging cushions, drifting around the place whilst intermittently smoothing out the creases in her white satin dress. When she found herself unexpectedly at the intercom and heard Miles's voice saying, "Hello darling, it's me," she wondered how she'd got there. It was like being woken from a powerful but indistinct dream. Only then did she remember what all the preparation had been for. She buzzed him in.

He entered and walked into the living room. He found her, Anna, sat on the far side of their much-changed lounge, her legs tucked beneath her, buoyed up and bolstered by the plush, red-leather armchair that had been her father's favourite seat. He looked around at all the candles and said, "Christ. It's like your about to perform a bloody funeral," which she thought both strange and apt. Strange, because whoever heard of a funeral held at night? They took place during the day, often in fairly drab spaces. They were usually naturally lit and, but for sparse decoration, had no real need of candles. Most ceremonies she'd attended kept macabre symbolism to a minimum and were washed with pale daylight, partly, she reckoned, to gird our mortal souls against the dark reality we are bound to witness and partly because priest work is a day job, too, after all. No, what

Miles was thinking of was a sacrifice. It felt apt, too, however, his clumsy misnomer, because she had been thinking all day about Spock. She had been thinking about him more and more, recently; her mind lingering on certain memories or instances. Like the way she had lain with him at the very end. Or the little ceremony after. There had been candles then.

She motioned with her glass of wine for Miles to sit on the sofa opposite her, which he did. She had placed the sofa squarely on the other side of the large, paisley rug, where usually there stood an oak coffee table, removed now for this special occasion. She wanted Miles to have some space to move around. Miles shifted in his seat, looked around a little nervously, and went to speak again, but Anna lifted a finger to her mouth and kissed it gently. She wanted him quiet. He seemed to gather this, peered over at her guiltily, smiling from behind his fringe and nodded.

Anna stood up. She walked across the room and behind Miles, to the light switch in the hall, where he had just come in. He didn't turn around to look at her, which she sort of liked. She stayed there for a moment, behind him, hoping he felt nervous, then she flicked the switch, and the light in the kitchenette came on. A bowl of milk had been placed on the tiled floor, between the breakfast bar her mother would have hated and the black granite work surfaces, all of which had been Miles's choice. She floated back to her seat. She sat down and drew her legs up under herself again.

"Shussshh," she said. "Shusssh. Look. You need to drink your milk."

Miles got down on all fours.

"Come on, sweetheart," said Anna. "Come on. Won't you drink a little bit of milk?"

She moved Spock to the very edge of his basket, feeling his small, warm, fragile ribcage rattle and heave beneath her touch. She pushed the bowl of milk under his nose, then lay down close to him, bringing her face close to his, and kissed his whiskered mouth as it wheezed the rank breath of decay. She didn't seek to move away. She reached around with her left hand, resting her forearm against the length of his body, and cradled his head in her palm. She took her thumb and moved it smoothly over his nose, stroking it from the spot of white to the space between his ears, in the way that was always certain to make him purr with satisfaction. He did not purr now. His eye lids flickered, and his breath stayed shallow and reedy. She kissed his nose again and felt his weak lungs rattle once more against her slender wrist.

Outside her door, her mother and father were bickering. Her mother had wanted to take the cat to the vet, so that they could, "Have it dealt with". Her father had stopped her, partly, Anna knew, because of the expense. "What's the bloody point?" he had said, "It won't even last the night." He would later claim he had done it for Anna, keeping her cat at home with her for its last night, but they all knew that was bollocks. She had heard what he had said. She remembered. But then, in that moment, she would not believe it was the end. She thought, if she could only get her cat to drink.

"Come on, darling, you need to drink your milk," said Anna.

He dipped his black head to the dish and lapped at it obediently. After tasting it a little he lifted his head in her direction and looked at her. He had that stupid, suggestive grin on his face, as though he thought this was something kinky, something sexual. It wasn't. Not yet anyway, and maybe not ever again. That was what she needed to find out. She stood and walked over to where he crouched, hunched awkwardly over the bowl.

"No, not like that, Miles," she said tersely, and pushed his head down so that his nose crashed into the saucer and he jerked his head back instinctively.

"Fucking hell, Anna!" Miles went to complain, but she shushed him again. He had milk all over his angry face. He looked like a very silly boy. The sight of him, along with the muffled shrieks of drunken girls walking the promenade outside, made her smile.

"You know the deal, Miles," she said, standing over him, raking her nails over his scalp in the way she knew he liked, "*every*thing I say." He dipped his head to the dish again.

She lifted the dish a little and tipped it so that she could pour a small amount of liquid into her cat's mouth. Spock did not move, his tongue sagged limply at the base of his open mouth and he made no attempt to swallow. The milk passed over his dry tongue, through his yellow teeth, and soaked into the pillow beneath his head. A lump of sadness suddenly balled in Anna's throat, but she forced it down. It hardened into anger in her stomach and she took the saucer in hand and tipped it viciously over the cat's snout.

"Drink, Spock! Come on," she shouted, "Just drink it! Stop being silly!"

The cat did not move. The milk washed over his mouth and his nose, soaking his fur. A small gurgling sound came from his throat, but he would not drink. Eventually, one eye blinked meekly as a register of distress and this was enough to break her. She scooped Spock up in her arms, held him to her chest, and started to rock him back and forth.

"Shusshhhh," She said, over and over, fat ugly tears rolling down her cheeks. "Shush now, it's okay."

With the milk still on her cat's face, Anna reached into her pocket and brought out the small length of twine she'd been keeping for this occasion. It was from that day on The Cob. She had found it again quite by accident but had put it aside, without knowing exactly what she would do with it. Now, she understood what it was for. She took it out and attached it to her cat's collar, then she walked across the room and he followed. It was time.

She sat down in her chair, the chair that was once her father's, with her obedient cat at her feet. She reached her right arm down the steep side of the worn red leather. She brought it back up, holding another plate. This plate was larger and was livid with a heap of reddish-purple lumps that shimmered repulsively in the candlelight. She held the plate there in front of her; a metallic, iodine smell sponged into the air as the slick, wet surfaces of the coarsely chopped liver quivered in front of her cat's twitching nose. She pushed the plate closer to his face. He seemed to recoil a little, then gave a small involuntary gag, but he did not move away.

"Eat," she said, and waited.

He looked at her through his fringe, his sad eyes not appealing for anything now except mercy, pity.

"Eat," she said again, and watched with a kind of detached amazement as Miles opened his mouth and began to nip at a sliver of slick purple meat, tugging at it with his front teeth, trying to haul it back into his mouth and swallow without chewing. He managed one piece, then the second made him retch. He put his face back to the plate again, but he suddenly sagged, flopped to one side and started to cry. Hiding his face from her, he let his silly fringe cover his face, like a sorry stage curtain over a broken clown.

"I'm sorry, Anna," he said. "Oh god, I don't... I'm just so sorry..."

It sounded genuine. His sobbing sounded real, from a place of real hurt. She put the plate down on the floor and opened her legs a little. She, Anna, let him move close to her so he could rest his head against the inside of her knee and cling to her like a child. She let him do this, though she felt nothing. Something terrible was hardening inside her and she felt numb. He pressed his face closer to her thigh and his tears dripped onto her knee and trickled down her pale shin. She pulled him even closer and began to stroke him, to stroke his hair, all the time staring blankly ahead of her.

She ran her hand over his black head, stroking and soothing. She kept saying, "Shush. Hush now. Shushhh. It's okay. It's going to be okay." But she knew herself that was not true. The cat was already dead.

Help

When Reinhold Bienemann describes the anatomy of a bee, its ocelli and gena, the unsurpassed utility of its tarsal claw, it is as though he is unfurling, through the weighted reverence of his words, some essential set of secrets about life itself, which, could you only clutch them to you just as he has, would exponentially deepen your understanding of the cosmos and the true nature of all things. Which may very well be the case. I'm just not that hot on bees.

It is the same when he delineates the finer qualities of Kölsch as compared to standard German pils, or extricates the mysteries of Hessisch folkloric literature. His tender probing, delicate disrobing and sweet, agonised exposure of his topic has such a sensual quality that those with a passing interest in psychoanalysis might detect another of the octogenarian's lifelong predilections: sex – in all its forms and majesty.

You see, eighty-year-old Reinhold Bienemann, as well as being a retired teacher, an amateur melittologist, semi-professional beekeeper, one-time state cycling champion, near-permanent university undergraduate and skilled artisanal craftsman specialising in wooden canoes – is a sex addict. Or rather, *was*. A former and not entirely reformed sex addict.

None of which is particularly pertinent to the story I am about to tell you now, except in an incidental, giving you a sense of the whole, sort of way. But I like to tell it anyway. Because it is, like him, amusing. What is most important to say about Reinhold Bienemann is that he is lovely. Or perhaps *was* is right here too? I haven't seen him in more than a year. But he is or was one of the nicest men I have ever met, that's a fact, and I feel glad to know or have known him. I must give him a call soon.

I had the pleasure of meeting Reinhold through a common acquaintance, Dagmarawit Awaferki. I know. Another impressive name. Attached to a very impressive lady. Move abroad and start trying to scratch up communities that you might fit into and, I promise you, you'll turn up more impressive names, almost always with people attached to them, than you know what to do with.

When I met Dagmarawit, I had been in Cologne for less than a year and to arrest the moral decay of my socialistic soul, I had sought out a voluntary position teaching English to emigrants under the auspices of the Red Cross. My day job was in a private school for posh kids – and whilst the dough was delightful, I was assaulted constantly by my guilt-laden need to balance a professed commitment to free, universal education with the daily business of being a parasitic, corporate shill. But anyway. This story is not about me or my many compromises. It is about the two lovely people I knew or know, depending on how you look at it: Dagmarawit and Reinhold. It is their story – I am just glad to be in the position to tell it.

Dagmarawit Awaferki, twenty-five years old, came to Germany from Eritrea. She had finally arrived in the late summer of 2015 via Ethiopia, Sudan, Libya, Greece, Bulgaria, Croatia, Northern Italy, Croatia again (returned), Slovenia, Austria and the Czech Republic, via land and sea and land and sea and land apparently without end, at just about that same time as I was entering the country quite comfortably on an aeroplane via a direct flight from Manchester, England.

She had made the move for much the same reasons as me – life seemed a bit shit and she really needed a change – although again, there is at least a degree or two of moral relativism at work in that description of things. For myself, a bit shit had meant a self-inflicted slide into financial difficulty, the recent end of a relationship and the acceleration of a blossoming alcohol addiction – but for Dagmar it meant abject poverty, an almost total lack of opportunity or education, the recent disappearance of her father – a political dissident – and the very real threat of detention and torture in one of many subterranean jails for her unwillingness to denounce her father and his friends for the crimes she did not believe they were guilty of and barely understood anyway. So, yes, the same but different. It should be fairly clear who had the inalienable legal right to seek refuge in Germany and start a new life. Me, of course. The drunk. Dagmarawit's residency and asylum status were under constant, niggardly review.

At about the time I got to know her, the January of 2016, Dagmarawit, whose name quite fortuitously could be shortened to the uber-traditional German name of Dagmar, which delighted her more than I understood, had been in Cologne for six months. She had been housed throughout that time in temporary accommodation in Ehrenfeld. She would spend another two years there before being relocated. It was a single room with bathroom cubicle in a drab-looking, two-storey rectangular prefab building which housed forty other refugees from different parts of the Middle East and North Africa. There were five more prefabs exactly like it on the complex, with more than two hundred people in total living in a relatively small space, but managing it, by and large, like my friend: with poise, patience and dignity.

Our meetings would happen in her room, which was kept always in a meticulous state of order, despite the cramped conditions. They were unfailingly accompanied by a cup or two of Eritrean tea, *Shahee*, which to my great regret I never thought to take the recipe for, though I'd watched its loving preparation many times. It was through these meetings, one hour per week every Wednesday, that I came to know Reinhold.

Reinhold was another of Dagmar's voluntary *Nachhilfe* teachers. His lessons – he taught German, *natürlich* – directly followed on from my own and after one or two fumbled half introductions in the corridors of Dagmarawit's lodgings, we got to chatting on an afternoon when Dagmar had needed to cancel Reinhold's session suddenly because of the onset of migraine. She had suffered these pains regularly since settling in Germany and though, as an ordinarily rational being, I felt her reasoning to be suspect, she attributed them directly to her distance from home, which somehow made sense to the part of me that rationality didn't rule.

Unbothered by the abrupt cancellation and in his usual high spirits, Reinhold trundled me off-site, pushing his vintage bicycle and explaining in his gravelly, impressive English why Germany really was, in his humble opinion, one of the greatest countries on God's green earth, some notable boot-clad missteps aside. We quickly arranged to meet at a *Brauhaus* the next evening so he could expound the many virtues of my new home in the kind of forensic detail that I would soon learn to be his trademark. We met as arranged and we drank and laughed like drains and before long he became a kind of personal cultural attaché – guiding my assimilation into *Kölnisch* culture – which to my incredulous delight centred around several, booze-soaked festivals. We would meet up nigh-on every week. In a matter of months, we must have drunk in every traditional Brauhaus in Cologne – and there are hundreds – but as I said, this story is not about me, or even us, really; it is about them: Dagmarawit and Reinhold. So now, if you'll let me, I will try to tell the story I sat down to write.

On the afternoon of May 4th, I had just finished my lesson with Dagmar and was hoping to collar Reinhold on my way out of the Red Cross complex. I lingered by the security desk, *quatsching* with the guard before collecting my ID, fully expecting the old dog with his characteristic hunch and baldpate to appear at any moment, pushing that beautifully maintained, bright blue bicycle of his. It was a warm and sticky afternoon. My brow prickled with sweat as I fought off the desire to head directly to some shady kiosk or *kneipe* and slake my raging midweek thirst. You see, I was still guarding some residual, though dwindling, regret from the weekend prior.

Like the good comrades we were, Reinhold and I had just celebrated International Workers' Day together on the previous Sunday and I had been unable to find my spare pair of glasses since. The city had buzzed all week with more suggestions of inappropriate sexual conduct from a small number of Muslim men during the festivities: touching and groping and the like; a kind of milder repeat of the New Year outrage that had just passed and made international headlines. The relocation of my drinking glasses notwithstanding, I was hoping to discuss this rumbling controversy with my wise old friend and, more pertinently perhaps, I hoped to tempt him into another Thursday night soirée in our favourite Brauhaus, Walfisch, by the Rhein. One more night of abstinence was quite enough, I reckoned, for any penance to my wretched super-ego to be fully paid. They did a delicious Kellerbier at Walfisch that was a little darker than the usual Koelsch and I could almost taste its sweet, yeasty coolness as I tapped my watch by the security guard´s corrugated porta-cabin. I hung around for fifteen minutes, itching with impatience, but he did not arrive, and so I jumped on my own rented bike and wheeled sourly back to the boarding lodge at my little-Englander's private school, roundly miffed.

Dagmar was also becoming, far more gracefully and forgivingly, aware of Reinhold's uncharacteristic lateness. She was busy too, however, for she was setting about a very important task. It was quite impolite, in Dagmarawit's world view, to serve two sets of guests from the same pot of tea. So, between my departure and Reinhold's arrival, she would always go through the process of preparing a fresh batch of *Shahee* from scratch – and I had watched her do it on occasions – with great care and concentration, as though the exact manner of its making was the critical ingredient for a satisfactory end product. Which I'm sure it was. That amount of love and attention has to add something, wherever it's applied.

Dagmar was a small, slight woman with long, braided black hair, dark brown skin and the measured, almost rehearsed movements of an actress playing an abbess. She had large, friendly brown eyes, which, nevertheless, often looked tired due to her heavy upper eyelids, and which she blinked slowly at seemingly deliberate intervals. She had thick, Frida Kahlo-style eyebrows, which also added something to the sense of a woman always in, if not thought, then meditation.

A deeply religious woman, Dagmar was part of the majority Orthodox Tewahedo Christian community in her native land of Eritrea, for all that had helped her family. When she made tea it was as though she was engaged in a small act of worship. First, she measured the leaves into an infuser, dropping the metal ball into the glass pot of hot water delicately and tying the metal chain to the handle. Next, she measured and ground a series of spices and herbs in a grey stone mortar, before decanting these into a smaller cup and adding water so that it formed a rich, brown paste. Next she sliced up a square inch of fresh ginger, carefully removing all the ecru rind, and dropped this into the pot. Finally, she stirred small amounts of the paste into the tea with one teaspoon in her right hand, whilst tasting small drops of the mixture with another in her left to check the balance was exactly right. When she was finally satisfied with the flavour, she placed the spoons in the sink, carried the pot to the table with two hands, sat down, nodded and smiled.

When alone in these quiet, in-between moments, Dagmar usually let her thoughts settle on God, or on her sister, who she thought of as being very much part of the same thing. If God was love, and she believed that to be true; a total love, then that must certainly include her sister, whom she loved above all else.

Dagmar's sister, Awate, was older by two years. In her short life, she had been all things to Dagmar: friend, exemplar, protector, teacher, mother and finally – or this was at least how Dagmar had come to view her sister's role in her own flight from Eritrea – saviour. It was Awate who had sourced the two-thousand-euro equivalent fee, from her own painstakingly assembled savings, that was used to extricate Dagmar from her home country.

Dagmar closed her eyes and thought of her sister's face. Proud, broader than her own, and starkly beautiful, the thought of Awate was in itself a kind of prayer, with all the yearning, love and reverence that implies. She gave the thought time and attention. She never rushed it. She listened to the special, busy quality of foreign stillness outside her window as her sister's face hung, veil-like, between her past and her present. The stillness of the moment was punctuated by the excited shrieks of children playing in the makeshift yard outside – the accommodation housed many families – and the rumbling of the S-Bahn line in the near distance. When she was done, she opened her eyes, and saw that the clock above her door said five fifteen, which was decidedly late for Reinhold, especially given his penchant for that most stereotypical of German qualities, *pünktlichkeit*.

It was often the case that we, Dagmar and I, would hear Reinhold approaching her room together, a little before five, as he routinely arrived before I was done with my session. "Die Hilfe, die Hilfe, die Hilfe kommt," he would chirrup in the corridor – and we would smile at each other and roll our eyes. As a well-travelled man who had journeyed extensively in the States in the seventies, Reinhold knew exactly what he was doing with this turn of phrase. The connotations of that term, the help, to denote him, the white man, and the irony of that, were important to him. A badge of honour, in fact. But Dagmar was oblivious. She took it, stylistically, as an amusing idiosyncrasy of this strange but pleasant old man and in terms of meaning, for just exactly what it meant: help, which she needed and was very glad to have.

There was only one occasion when Dagmar's lesson with Reinhold had not taken place in her little room – and that had become one of her most treasured memories of her newly adopted home. On that day, Reinhold had called ahead to explain that, due to a cycling mishap, he was nursing a bruised hip, and didn't think he was up to the hour-long round trip between his home in Deutz and the Ehrenfeld complex. He wondered, however, if it was allowed that Dagmar visit him. At pains not to breech any security requirements, he emailed Dagmar his address as well as copies of his Aúsweis and the assurance that his wife, Lydia, would also be at home in her office, where she worked as a Psychoanalyst. He left out the fact that his wife, some twenty years his junior, specialised in treatment of sex addiction, or that he had once been one of her clients, but he did let it be known he had a pretty decent range of teas to offer too. Dagmar accepted the offer gratefully and made her way across town.

Stepping into the large and stylishly furnished townhouse of Herr Bienemann was genuinely like entering another world for Dagmar. In her short time in Germany, she had seen many a grand building, but the interiors of those bureaucratic palaces were stripped down and functional, whitewashed and imposing, intentionally soul-sappingly drab. To be invited into the home of a retired European professional was to at least begin to understand what was meant by those outdated, though all too revealing, terms: First and Third World.

Reinhold's home smelled fantastic. The lingering aroma of good bread, aged leather and well laundered fabrics permeated everything. It was an ordered home, without being impeccable. The house had that effortlessly at-ease-with-itself quality that seems to be the calling card of the intellectual middle classes. A well-thumbed hardback on the arm of an armchair, earthenware sculptures out of Dagmar's home continent standing proudly on shelves of finely crafted German oak. Any shabbiness existed only on account of so many items being literally antique and of the sheer quantity of treasures Reinhold had accrued. It was like a museum, to Dagmar. A museum of unreal life.

Good Herr Bienemann had not anticipated his visitor's sense of wonder. He was instantly embarrassed not to have guessed how she might feel to find herself amongst such unassuming plenty. But he was not phased. Reflexively as a deft grey cat, he abandoned any intention of following the stuffy lesson on the four cases that he had prepared for the evening, and seeing how Dagmar's eyes were drawn particularly to the smattering of family photographs proudly adorning his home's many nooks, dressers and walls, he pulled out a stack of family albums from one of the shelves and invited Dagmar to peruse at her own leisure.

The man was never more animated than when talking about family, particularly his own. I don't know how many times I myself was shown videos of various grandchildren doing unspectacular things to the accompaniment of mind-blown commentary from their outlandishly proud Opi. To Reinhold, children really were the most spectacular thing in existence, better even than the act of getting them, which was saying something for him. He tended Dagmar's every hesitant and broken question with the wild delight of an enthusiastic tour guide. Names, dates, memories, buildings, occasions; all these were not just furnished but festooned with laughing, loving detail. By the end of the evening, Dagmar had learned and used more German than she'd thought she was capable of, and three hours had passed by seemingly in an instant. Though she had been in the country for almost a year and had received many kindnesses in that period from assorted officials and strangers, only now did she know what it meant to be truly welcomed.

Printed photographs, Dagmar sought to explain, were rare in her homeland, hence her particular fascination. She kept a small cache on her mobile phone which she would sometimes idly scan, but the tiny cardboard box her family kept of scattered memories were so incredibly precious, she had felt like a thief when she accepted two or three prints from the family collection for her protracted journey across Europe. The photos, which all included Awate, of course, now sat in her own battered shoebox of keepsakes, stashed beneath her single bed in Ehrenfeld. She promised herself in that moment that she would find the money to buy some decent frames for their display just as soon as she could. Seizing on the moment, Reinhold hollered for his wife and insisted that Lydia take a photo of himself and Dagmar together, arms over one another's shoulders, like old, tea drinking buddies. The night ended and they said warm goodbyes. Dagmar had run the night through many times in her head since, smiling or laughing to herself at her teacher's unimpeachable hospitality, but she had never once thought to ask what had become of the photo Lydia made.

Now, back in her room with the clock ticking, Dagmar had a choice in front of her. She could accept Reinhold's uncharacteristic no-show with the shrug of indifference that seemed commonplace in the busy lives of her European hosts, or she could listen to the growing disquiet in her displaced heart and set out, uninvited, to pay her old friend an impromptu visit. Picking up her coat, which she still wore throughout the summer months on Awate's insistence, stuffing her mobile phone into one of the pockets, she exited the bedsit and made her way towards Wolfsohnstrasse Bahnhof.

On the rumbling U-Bahn ride through the city, one that she usually enjoyed, Dagmar shot Reinhold a few clipped, exploratory text messages, but receiving nothing back from the tech savvy senior, her concern started to grow. As well it might have, because it was just at the point that Dagmarawit was grabbing her things and striding out of her own flimsy front door in Ehrenfeld, that Reinhold Bienemann was slumping into the most dangerous phase of a bee sting induced anaphylactic shock. After the rapid initial swelling of his lips and tongue, the anaphylaxis was now extending to his airways, slowly but surely choking out oxygen and causing the veteran beekeeper to fall to the ground and lie prone on the shaggy lawn of his pleasantly sunlit garden.

Dagmar stepped off the U4 in Seuvenstrasse and immediately asked directions from a tattooed youth in a tight hooded top. Getting her bearings and heading in the direction he had pointed her, she began muttering Tigrinyan prayers under her breath, the eerie sense that something might be very wrong growing with every step. The coat had been a mistake; she started to sweat profusely. She took it off and tied it round her waist, but even her long white and blue Habesha felt heavy on her shoulders now. The sweat ran from her forehead and into her eyes. Wiping one arm across her brow, she lifted the crushed white cotton of her dress awkwardly up to her knees, gathering it over her elbow, and broke into a jog.

By this point, Reinhold's own vision had started to fail. Flailing and gasping, he saw surges of black and red occlusions pass across his quickly tunnelling field of vision, as the inflamed flesh in his trachea began to flush with an unhelpfully thick layer of histamine-triggered epithelial mucus. It was a process Reinhold understood well. He was entirely conversant with the biological imperatives that drove the sequence of enzymatic reactions he was currently experiencing. But none of that knowledge could help him now. He was entering fatal territory and losing consciousness quickly. Reinhold Bienemann was on borrowed time.

It should come as no surprise, of course, that an educated man like Herr Bienemann should have been so well informed of the physiological impact of anaphylaxis. He was extensively well read in a range of sciences outside his numerous areas of niche interests, but there was, nevertheless, a specific reason why he was something of an expert on anaphylactic shock. You see, there is another important thing you need to know about Reinhold to get the full sense of the moment and the man. He had once recounted to me, over a gallon or two of Koelsch, how he had long fancied the art of beekeeping, but had put it off until old age, finally taking up the hobby at the age of sixty. The fascination with apiary had started early, it being in his bloody name, after all – *Biene*, in German, means *bee* – but he explained how he'd been too timid in his youth to give it a try. Reinhold as a timid youth was about as unconvincing a spectre as I'd ever been presented, and I think I may have actually laughed in his face, but he explained to me that there was a good reason for this trepidation – Reinhold was allergic to bee stings. Seriously allergic. One sting had the effect of making his flesh within a ten-centimetre radius balloon enormously; two or more could incapacitate him and, without fairly urgent medical assistance, kill the man in hours. He had discovered the allergy at the age of ten, when a single sting on the neck had rendered him unconscious and bedridden for more than a day. You might therefore have imagined that beekeeping as a pastime would have rapidly and lastingly lost its appeal, but not so. For Reinhold Bienemann, progression into old age seemed to be one gloriously extended exercise in confounding expectations.

Far from taking the well-trodden path of shrinking into a fearful, diminished husk of his former self, Reinhold had chosen to contour his seniority with more faces than the mirror balls of the fetish clubs he still attended. It said everything about the man that, with this history of fairly severe allergies, including an understandable aversion to potentially fatal bee stings, he should voluntarily take up, in later life, the very specific hobby of keeping hundreds of thousands of actual bees. And expertly, too. His honey was delicious. It sold at twenty euros a jar under the label Reinhold's Glory. It really was as though, on seeing the glinting tip of Father Time's scythe on the horizon, Herr Bienemann had decided to assault the Reaper's approach with a series of premeditated, inflammatory gestures – a wild, unbridled goading of sorts – as though daring death to come and have a go if he foolishly believed he was hard enough.

This time, it seemed, death fancied his chances. As Reinhold lay prone and gobbing in his bee-keeping get-up, like some fat-lipped, Hazmat suited guppy – it appeared as though time was about to be finally called. And, typical of the man, his mind did not race with the kaleidoscopic cavalcade of regrets, triumphs, sexual escapades and/or treasured poignancies available to him – no, he was thinking about his queen. He was fairly sure that what had started the disquiet in his hive and had subsequently led to the potentially fatal series of stings on his face and neck, was the building of an emergency cell. Emergency cells, when they appear in hives, almost always indicate the premature replacing of an established queen. This is bad, because it indicates ill health in a queen, and by extension, the entire colony. Ill health was something Herr Bienemann had so far been adept at avoiding, in himself and his bee colony, so it bothered him. Deeply. He hoped earnestly that he could survive his current – rather serious – health scare, so that he could investigate the matter with the fullness it demanded. And that was the last clear thought he had, before everything went black.

When Dagmarawit arrived at Reinhold's home, some five minutes later, she could still hear what remained of the life and death drama between queen and keeper fizzling out in the garden behind his home. Alerted by the low buzzing sound, she eschewed a period of doorbell interrogation that might have cost Herr Bienemann his life, and proceeded straight to the rear of the house, where she saw Reinhold, stricken. Frau Bienemann, as it happened, was deeply indisposed at that very moment in a sort of research orgy across town, so that the doorbell, were Dagmar to have tried it, would have gone asphyxiatingly unanswered for quite some time.

Acting out of a mix of instinct and half-remembered teachings from a long-dead aunty about snake bites, Dagmar set about saving Reinhold's life. She dropped to her knees, batting off a few irritating drones who might have really finished poor Reinhold off, and began to suck at the stings still lodged in the ballooned protuberances of flesh on his face and neck. She spat them onto the lush green grass and checked for more stings. Finding none, she pushed him onto his side, tilted back his head and then called the emergency services number she had memorised on her first day in Germany: one, one, two. A vital piece of knowledge that she'd always expected to need for herself.

She explained, then, with the few words of German she had, words Reinhold had helped her to learn, what had happened to the man she called her teacher. Fighting down her desperation, she said the words "biene", "angriff", "keine artmen", "bitte kommen schnell, bitte kommen schnell." She explained as best she could, with an unnatural level of composure, given the circumstances, what had happened. She gave the address as clearly as she was able. Then, breathless herself, she took Reinhold's hand, lay back in the grass and thanked God for His guidance. She closed her eyes against the early evening sun, seeing her sister's smiling face as she did and, still sweating, she prayed.

***

When Dagmar showed me the story in the newspaper cuttings, some weeks later, I was both amazed and irritated. Amazed at the unthinkingly modest, spontaneous heroism of this collected young lady – but irritated when I noted how Dagmar was referred to as asylum seeker or refugee in every single scrap of text that she passed to me. She said she did not mind and, clearly, she meant it.

"Refugee saves Retired Teacher's Life." "Asylum seeker heroically saves beekeeper, 80," and so on. I tried my pompous, patronising best to explain just why I was irritated on her behalf, but to no avail. Put me in her shoes, I explained, and it would have been "Englishman saves," or "Expat teacher", but she smiled so calmly as to make my ire seem childish. It was just another of those moments that left me in awe of her. Her unaffected poise. The ease of her equanimity. Or perhaps, I mean it is possible, that she really didn't understand what I was blathering on about. She always says I talk too quickly and say too much. I guess she has a point.

"All that matters is that God is good," she told me then. I told her I didn't agree. "*You* are good, Dagmar. *You* made the difference." She shook her head, and I had the clear sense she was about to say something immensely profound, when we heard from the corridor, "Die Hilfe, die hilfe, die hilfe kommt…" We smiled at each other and rolled our eyes.

In her room, after I had left, Reinhold sipped *Shahee* and regretfully informed Dagmar that the session that afternoon would be their last as teacher and student. His near-death experience had taught him one thing clearly, he told her, and that was that in order to go on improving in the field, he would need to collect a great deal more knowledge on the science and secrets of beekeeping from a much wider, global range of sources. He had therefore made the decision to travel directly to New Jersey, in time for the Eastern Apicultural Society Convention of Beekeepers in July and begin an American Tour of the beekeepers´ convention circuit, that might also serve the function of allowing him to revisit some old friends and haunts established on his one prior trip, back in 1972. *She* had inspired him to do this, he said. He thanked her for that, leaving out the fact that he would be taking two suitcases, each with very different specialist equipment. Many of those friends and haunts from his original trip had been from the quite different, though sometimes intersecting, community of *enthusiasts*, but in a way that was quite unlike Reinhold, he decided to keep that fact for himself.

So that was that. He was recommitting himself to studenthood. Any meet ups they arranged from then on, he said, with a glint in his eye, would have to be purely as friends. He hugged her warmly, thanked her again from his heart, then reaching into a plastic bag he had been carrying inconspicuously at his side, he put down a large, untitled leather clad album on her table, next to their emptied *Shahee* cups. Dagmar went to say something, but Reinhold lifted a finger to his lips and made his way theatrically to the door on accentuated tip toes like an exiting cartoon villain. He waved a silent goodbye and left the room.

Dagmar closed the door behind her guest, shook her head and sighed. She emptied the tea pot of *Shahee* and tidied the worktops of all the clutter. She moved around her small room, patiently tending to this and that, putting things back where they belonged, while the serious looking leather book smouldered at her from her little kitchen table, always at the edge of her vision. Finally, she cleared the table too, putting the cups into the sink, so that the book stood alone, and she could open the broad pages their full width. She turned the cover page. She smiled. Inside, it contained, as she had guessed it would, just one photo. It was the photo of herself and Reinhold, from that night in his home, sitting on his sofa, beaming, arm in arm. Above, Reinhold had written the title, in exquisitely ornate golden lettering, *Für Familie und Freunde*. Dagmar smiled again, then bent below the bed. She brought out her little box and began.

The Managed Decline

The Somerset Room, with all its oak-panelled formality, really made the perfect location for a public inquiry. It was large but cramped, regal in that direst, medieval sense. The long, thin room had low ceilings so that, when all the required trappings of a judicial undertaking were factored in – the desks, benches and galleries, the files and fittings, the cameras and the sheer number of people – it felt intensely claustrophobic. It was warm too. Like many a space in Westminster, it was Grade I listed, so modern air conditioning could not be fitted without a horribly expensive palaver and therefore it *made* you sweat. Perfect, Brandwood had often thought it. Countless times, in fact, over the past god-knew-how-many years, watching some poor fucker squirm. The thought squitted back to him now with pancreatic bitterness as he dabbed his brow beneath the hot yellow lights, wishing to be anywhere other than where he was, but most of all wishing he could go home and sleep.

Of course, he wouldn't go home or sleep, not for some time yet. There were far too many things he was obliged to do beyond perspiring here for another hour or more, answering any number of these ridiculous fucking questions. Brandwood bit the soft, newly ulcerating flesh behind his bottom lip and pretended to concentrate. Sweat pooled and cooled in itchy creases. Could he remember being present when such and such a document was drafted? Did he know who might have been present at such a meeting over such a topic? Could he recall a certain fucking configuration of words about some obscure Northern town in a discussion from nineteen eighty-fucking-six? He had been well briefed and played the game on autopilot: Be as vague and polite as possible. Incriminate, if you must, only the fallen and the weak.

He picked at a flaky nail on his ring finger and wondered about fungal infections. For the third time in his life, a toenail had blistered and shed like a winter leaf and he wondered if it could be the start of something catching. Now this thing had started happening on his hands. They were most likely unconnected though. The toe-nail debacle had happened before, and always the same nail, on the middle toe of his left foot and with decades between their incidence. This thing with his hands, dry skin and cracked nails, it was new. He was entering the final year of his fifties; he'd be fifty-nine in a week. He was getting used to parts of his body rebelling or even giving up entirely. From the throbbing near his sphincter, he guessed it would be his prostate that mutinied next.

His mobile phone spazzed in his pocket, which brought into focus the prickly discomfort of his ball sack. Why did otherwise well-fitted suit trousers have to be so tight around the crotch when you sat?

"I should have a word with my tailor," he thought, and started shifting impatiently in his seat, trying to wriggle a pocket clad finger into the angry fold of his groin for some surreptitious relief. Dame Williamson, that acerbic old cow, clocked it instantly.

"I'm sorry if we seem to be making you uncomfortable, Mr James?" she said, mugging slyly for the cameras, enjoying it.

"Not at all," said Brandwood, smiling angelically back at her. That bitch. She loved this. It was all that she lived for now she'd sloped off to the Lords and stopped being in any real way relevant. She came alive again in these fucking inquiries and the powers that be loved wheeling her out – literally, the woman had been confined to a wheelchair for the past half-decade – because of her famed *impartiality* and, of course, for *diversity*.

He knew without checking who the message was from. Brandwood had been having an affair of some kind or another for most of his married life, but this latest one had been going on two years and had come to feel like bloody matrimony in every way except those that were beneficial. His wife, God bless her, had long been happy with a kiss on the forehead at night and a regularly serviced credit card, but this one wanted all that and his fucking attention on top. It was a nightmare, but there didn't seem to be a way out. He'd picked badly, this time. His mistress was also his boss's wife.

Of course, she hadn't been when he'd started fucking her. Brandwood would not have dared being so remiss. Not again, anyway. No, back then his current boss had been a back-bench nobody – a laughing stock – but the way the government was cycling through *talent* it had perhaps been inevitable that he'd end up in the cabinet and now, by some absurd confluence of fuckwittery and chance, this man, the grade-A cunt, was Home Secretary. Yes, he was a mess and yes, he would probably be gone himself in a matter of months, but that didn't help Brandwood right at this moment when all he wanted to do was to tell this psychotic, cock-hungry harridan of his to stick her head in an oven and/or leave him alone.

His arsehole, as expected, started to tremble now, too. For around three months, Brandwood had been getting very sudden, rather bloody attacks of the shits. These "Raspberry Splatters", as one coarse junior official, Willis, had dubbed them, typically left the toilet bowl looking like a suicide bombing in a reinforced igloo. It had shocked him enough the second time to see his doctor and, after an agonisingly analogue examination, he had been sent to the proctologist and then on to oncology. He'd had a letter sitting on his hallway sideboard for the last fortnight but had been too busy to even think about it, what with preparing for the inquiry, then attending the inquiry, then preparing for the fucking inquiry again. There was no way he could finger his own anus in such plain public view, no matter how much he craved to, so he clenched his arse cheeks together and tried his upmost to focus on whatever Dame know-it-all was saying now.

"I really don't recall," he answered, "I was new to such meetings at the time. Impressed just to be there, quite honestly. It was something of a blur..."

In his pocket, as it spazzed again, a text was saying, "Brandy, I need you," or, "Brandy, I hate you," or something else entirely that meant the same fucking thing. He breathed in deeply and steeled himself. There was so much more of the night left to go.

***

Outside the Pavilion, the Thames side terrace bar of the Commons, Brandwood sucked on a Dunhill and finally took his phone out of his pocket. The view from where he stood, just ten yards or so above the level of the Thames and directly beneath the full erectile glory of Big Ben, was still a wonder to him. Lights danced on the shimmering black water in the same way they'd done for kings and queens a thousand years before. In this city, centuries of blood and stone lay, one on top of another, each entombing and immortalising the legends within. It was a fucking miracle, but a greedy one; it always needed more. The sheer size of it, ten million souls, needed sacrifice, human sacrifice, *his* sacrifice to keep it running. Brandwood's phone said eight p.m., but it also showed thirty-nine unread messages. Thirty-nine unread messages in three hours. For fuck's sake.

The normal gathering of egregious wankers had congregated on the terrace, but Brandwood was separate from them. He thought he'd spotted Peter from the Treasury, another one of the recently implicated, leering morosely over a red wine on his way in, but he'd avoided eye contact and strode straight through. He stood alone, off to the side, in a quiet spot smoking, sipping whisky and contemplating the myriad complications of his situation: his marriage, his job, his mistress, his son. They all required tending to, but this inquiry was consuming so much of his time that, even if he were minded to, he simply would not have had the time to address them all. Staring blankly down at his phone, he tapped the map icon and tried to focus on the problem in hand.

Eight o'clock and he needed to be in Shoreditch by nine. The roads would still be busy, but with two changes on the Tube and all that late-September pleb flesh in his way, he figured a black cab was still the way to go. He'd be an hour or so in The Dick and Sally being debriefed by the wanker of a lawyer that Geoffrey had set him up with, then on to the hotel in Islington they frequented at Lucricia's shrill insistence. He hated the place. It fucking stank of potpourri, which meant it was boutique, apparently. He'd have to pick up a gift on the way. An expensive bottle of wine and a bunch of flowers was the minimum expected at these trysts, come Hell or high water, both of which could be invoked anyway depending on which side of the bed she was growling from when he arrived. If Brandwood was lucky, he'd be with Lucy for ten thirty pm and, if she could be appeased, he might be in a cab home for half past midnight. This meant arriving home somewhere close to one thirty am, affording him a solid four hours in the guest room before the whole ghastly business started again. This imagined scenario was very much a best case. He swigged down the last of the whisky and grimaced.

Brandwood's head ached. He made a nodded gesture to the waiter hovering at the terrace door, who duly ducked inside. He knew he should really get moving, but he needed a little bit more fire in his belly first if he was going to do battle with the Dragon of Islington once more. Waiting for his next drink, he closed his eyes and sieved through the wiry hair of his large nostrils the light scent of trout farm that splashed up playfully from the river. Brandwood had always felt that rivers smelt like trout farms, ever since an early visit to one in the Cairngorms at the age of four. Of course, it would be more accurate or logical to say that trout farms smelt like rivers – given that rivers and aquatic life must necessarily have predated the emergence of farms of any kind, but this was not a concession that Brandwood's sense of order was prepared to make. He would go on, he felt sure, seeing it his way round until the day he died. When he opened his eyes again, he had the eerie sensation that he was being watched. His eyes darted about the terrace, and though all the groups seemed engaged in the same routine skulduggery as just a moment earlier, he couldn't shake the feeling that the atmosphere had changed. He felt watched, compromised. Exposed. Closing his eyes to think about trout farms amidst all these jostling cocks had been a mistake. He left cursing himself, without receiving his second drink.

There was a line of cabs waiting for Brandwood on the road abutting the north end of Westminster Abbey. Before stepping inside, he took the time to appraise his appearance in the sleek black flank of the Hackney carriage. Though his hair was thinning considerably and had been grey since forever, Brandwood felt, not entirely without reason, that his Roman nose, square jaw and close shave let him pass for a man in his forties. Something, certainly, still did the trick for the wives of Whitehall and it couldn't be money alone; there were plenty that were richer in the company he kept. He prodded the roll of fat that bulged over his belt line. His belly was getting rounder of late and, disturbingly, he couldn't think how it was related to his lifestyle. He still played squash twice a week and he wasn't drinking that much more than normal. He had to admit, however, that it was becoming unsightly. He was so preoccupied by his thoughts and the niggling discomfort by his bladder, that he almost missed completely the reflection, in the door panel at his feet, of another person. This beggar, propped against the railings of the ancient church, was so consumed within the pile of clothes they wore, that the sex was pretty much indeterminable, and their outstretched arm was almost entirely obscured. Brandwood tutted, jumped into the cab and gave the name of his destination, but his eyes lingered on that forlorn and lumpen form in the wing mirror until they rounded the corner on to the bridge, when Brandwood noticed, to his own surprise, that he was holding his breath.

Rounding the corner, clawing at the knot in his tie, he sighed deeply before catching sight of another two vagrants, squabbling over some find from a public bin outside the tube station. These old men, though dishevelled, did not look like the kind you'd expect to see combing the city streets, let alone fighting each other for its bounty. They had on unremarkable charity shop coats and one wore halfway respectable glasses. Their trousers were not torn or even, to the naked eye, stained.

"Come off it," thought Brandwood and scoffed to himself. Well, it had to be some kind of joke! A set up. A stunt. Brandwood often had the feeling that apparently random events were arranged just so, to hector or taunt him in some way. Things out there were rough for some, yes, he wasn't so detached from wider society as to miss that, but they were no worse than they had always been. On the streets of Chicago, or Calcutta, weren't such sights common? Hadn't it always been this way? Was he supposed to be drawing a connection between the goings-on in the Somerset Room, the details of which seemed so remote from the politics of the day as to be faintly absurd, and this street-side vision of social decay? Well, he wouldn't. And with this act of mental defiance, the sense of being watched returned once more. He flicked his eyes toward the rear-view mirror and saw that, indeed, the cabby was watching him, quite intently. Perhaps he recognised him from the papers or the rolling TV news. The inquiry had been getting a lot of coverage lately. "See?" thought Brandwood, "A simple causal explanation." Things happen incidentally. They don't have to mean anything bigger. They don't have to mean anything at all. He stared back aggressively at the cabby, who, rumbled, turned his attention back to the road.

***

The pub, The Dick and Sally, was heaving when Brandwood arrived, but he quickly spotted his wanker of a lawyer, Brinman, gamely shielding a pair of bar stools by a central pillar like some fat, bald frontiersman ensnared by native hipsters. The man was sweating profusely and gripping a pint of brown coloured beer. He looked decidedly out of place. Brandwood almost felt sorry for him, besieged as he was by much younger, more attractive examples of his species and their craft ales. It was a sentiment that evaporated the moment he'd reached the pillar and Brinman opened his fat, wanker mouth.

"You looked a fuckin' mess today," said Brinman, in place of hello.

"Thank you," said Brandwood. "I didn't know you cared. You look like shit right now, if we're comparing notes. And by the way, I did exactly as you instructed, so I don't know what you're complaining about."

"That's funny, I don't remember tellin' you to squirm around like a fuckin' slug on a fuckin' saxo patch. You looked fuckin' dodgy, is what I'm sayin'. Need to cut that out. But you answered fine, to be fair, what little I saw..."

Brinman, Brandwood knew, was from a village north of Oxford and had been to the same first-rate public school as his old pal Geoffrey, so this cockney twang was pure, wanker affectation. He did, however, have an uncanny knack for preempting Dame Williamson's line of questioning, some sort of wanker voodoo, so he was a necessary evil.

"What's the script tomorrow then? What are they likely to ask?" enquired Brandwood, eyes darting around the room, already eager to be through.

"Well, they've done with the meeting, you've dodged that bullet… well done. I reckon from now on it'll be documentation. Those memos. In your role back then, they'll know you had to have been involved in movin' 'em round, but that's all you give 'em, right? You weren't present when they were drafted. You never felt the slightest fuckin' sneak of curiosity to read what was in 'em. No, no, no, no, no, me lady. That's the fuckin' line."

"Right. Blanket denial. Seems simple enough."

"Yeah, but she'll peck ya. Be ready for that. She'll keep at it, trying to wrong foot you, you know? *'But you? An Oxford graduate? Completely in the dark? Surely not…'* Make you feel silly, like."

"I already feel silly," said Brandwood, then noticing the sharpening of Brinman's eyes, added, "but yes, yes. Sure thing. I'll be on my guard." For a man who spent such a large part of his time concocting laughable excuses, Brinman possessed a distinct lack of a sense of humour.

As his lawyer went on talking, Brandwood scanned the floor trying to remember where to find the gents. With his condition as it was, a sure and certain path to the WC was as essential as four walls when entering any room where he expected to stay for longer than ten minutes. It was almost impossible to see through the thick forest of beards and the stiff denim they bobbed on, but finally he spied some signage, a blended icon of the male and female gender signs, and snorted. He couldn't understand why any grown man would choose to conduct his business in a place so insufferably *relevant* as this. Brinman was too old, surely, to feel like he belonged. Brandwood, for one, felt completely alone. Then, feeling his stomach turn violently, he thought he recognised the face of his son in the crowd.

To his great relief it wasn't Milo, but Brandwood excused himself anyway. The digestive shock brought on by the potential, unexpected proximity of a family member had kick-started something that he would find hard to long contain. Elbowing his way through a throng of post-ironic preensters, he felt two things. The first was contempt. Brandwood knew from experience that a great many of these parentally dependent libertarians – these boudoir Bolsheviks, in his own, fondest denigration – would comprise the boardrooms of FTSE 100s and cabinet meetings of the not-too-distant future. He had spent too long second guessing their faddish voting intentions and defaming their demagogues to feel even a hint of sympathy for the sneering and privileged positions they assumed for themselves, lecturing his generation on the immorality of a system that had delivered them their solid gold lecterns from which to sermonise and that, once all the pennies started dropping, they'd happily be cradled by until their cosseted demise. The second feeling was regret. Regret that he could no longer see this demographic – and to Brandwood they really were just that – with anything other than enmity. He had been comfortable enough in this assumed state of mutual hostility, until it had become increasingly clear that his own son comprised one of their number.

In Milo, his and Elizabeth's only child, he had perplexingly sired another devotee to the allotment loving cultist currently leading her majesty's opposition. Brandwood was, officially, of course, neutral on all matters political – but his life's work had been in steering the ship on the most even keel despite the navigational nihilism of a uniformly potty ruling class. Now, against everything he'd thought he stood for – stability, pragmatism – his own son was backing the biggest lunatic of all, Old Greybeard, the fantasist in a flat cap, and using up his allowance buying bespoke protest props from banners4you. com. Even more embarrassingly, the internet site was listed on several of his recent Visa statements, which he had to submit for tax purposes.

He worried about Milo and the company he kept. He wondered where he was right now. In a bar, no doubt, with his comrades – drinking to their latest awareness raising stunt. For a boy, a man in fact – Milo was twenty-two after all – who professed such concern for the impending apocalypse, he drank as though complete oblivion were a rather welcome state. On this particular front, Brandwood could not entirely blame the lad. Just like his own father, Brandwood had drunk heavily since his teenage years and it hadn't held him back any. If anything, it was a social lubricant, though of course even in this, Milo had to take things to extremes. Being pleasantly soused just didn't seem to do it for M. James Esq., and Brandwood had lost count of the number of times he'd had to help his son off the hallway floor, all sixteen stone of him, and into a bed that would frequently end up pissed. Their housekeeper – what was her name? – God bless her, was worth her weight in gold. So, whilst Milo liked a drink and Brandwood wasn't *un*concerned – it was the politics he could not forgive. He could love a drunk, love an idiot, even, but he could not love a commie. It troubled him greatly.

Mercifully, the last patron was exiting the facilities when Brandwood entered the WC. At last, he was alone. His business, on so many fronts, seemed unpleasantly noisy at the moment, and this area was no exception. An audience, a mixed gender one at that, was the last thing he desired when he, all too frequently, dropped trou. He breathed a deep sigh of relief and inhaled the lemon scent of toilet cleaner like a blast of pure mountain air. The facilities, tiled green like an East End pie shop, were surprisingly clean. He chose the furthermost cubicle and disinfected the toilet seat with a small bottle of lotion that he kept in his jacket pocket. He released the biting tension of his belt, dropped his slacks and sat down squarely on the pot, the aged muscularity of his fleshy buttocks quivering with anticipatory tension. No sooner had his arse contacted plastic than the first wet blast was issued. An unholy intestinal stink quickly filled his booth, then spread out more widely to inhabit the room. A series of long, sonorous and sloppy farts followed, like the sounding of massive wet horns, as his distended bowel gave full voice to its glowering irritability. The arrangement was finalised by a number of now customary splatter claps, which usually marked the end of the bloody but short-lived affair. By this point a couple of other aghast visitants had joined him in the toilet block, but he no longer cared. As the boiled cabbage stench of his own shit rose gloriously around him, he felt the purest moment of peaceful release he'd known in weeks.

It could not last long. Summoning him from his shit-scented reverie was his very own miniature dick-kicker, pinging away in his pocket, signalling a sudden flurry of messages. He dragged his boss-eyed gaze away from the elaborately etched lady's part on the toilet door and opened the last of his incoming messages, mouthing the mutilated words to himself as he read them.

"If u r nt hr n 30 mns…"

Fuck, he thought. The threats had started. The vowel shorn, twitchy threats. It meant he had an hour tops before Lucricia went full Glenn Close. He flushed and cleaned up carefully, twice wiping the bowl and under the seat with sanitiser, before thoroughly sanitising his hands themselves and finally flushing away all evidence like a professional. Leave a place as though you were never there, his father had told him, though he wasn't entirely sure he'd meant it for this context. All the same, it was a maxim he'd tried and too often failed to live by. He checked his other messages. They were from the Home Sec's PA detailing a six thirty a.m. pre-briefing briefing that, apparently, he absolutely had to be at. It seemed to Brandwood strikingly unfair that he should have to fuck his boss's wife and keep up with his almost primordial schedule, but what could be done? He had to play the hand he'd been dealt. He pinged an Uber, washed his hands again, and went out to finish off with Brinman.

Attesting to the ordeal, the crowd had thinned out somewhat when he re-emerged from the toilets and Brinman had located them a booth better befitting their exceptional status. Brandwood collected two whiskies from the bar and proffered them instantly as a parting shot. Brinman wasn't quite done, but after some slightly theatrical synoptic instructions, he held up his glass like a fucking mafia don waited for Brandwood to clink his acquiescence. Brinman liked some ceremony to conclude their tedious little trysts and Brandwood was happy to indulge. He slugged back the whisky and within a minute he was in the street, dejectedly flagging down Japhet and his 2018 Honda Insight.

Japhet had four point nine stars on Uber and Brandwood could tell from the way his eyes twinkled in the rear-view mirror he probably earned them with his first-rate banter. Brandwood rubbed his neck, gave the address, mentioned the requisite drop point at the Tesco express adjacent the hotel and, seeking to nip any potential conversation in the bud, immediately asked for more volume on the radio, making out like it was a show he liked to catch. He regretted this a moment later when he heard the unmistakable voice of LBC's Toby O'Brainiac, reprising his bleeding heart bit about, "Lack of public trust in our elected officials." But what was he supposed to do: ask the guy to turn it down again? He'd look mad, so he just sat there, stewing.

He checked his watch. Again. He was partly concerned about Lucricia. Or rather, he was concerned about how *he* would fare *with* Lucricia. Although he sensed on some level she was thrilled by the caged tiger routine, he knew too well that the longer he made her wait for his arrival, the longer and more degraded would be the sexual catharsis required to assuage her. Having already achieved a halfway Zen-like state on the mixed gender shit-pot, he wasn't sure he still possessed the requisite filth within. But what irked him more, for all he tried to screen it out, was just why he was listening to pedantic notes of pug-nosed liberal Toby O'Brien, sniding through the stereo at him at nigh-on eleven in the evening? Didn't his show go out in the afternoon precisely so working people didn't have to listen to his part-time, post-breakfast moralising? He was, it transpired, a guest on some culture show or other, pushing his new book on good governance, as though any shit-eating talk show host would know the first thing about the mechanics of Westminster.

"Transparency," Tobes sobbed, was what was lacking at the heart of government. What a fucking wheeze. When had transparency ever been the primary concern of any organisation, or individual, for that matter, in the history of recorded time? Our secrets define us. Our successes, by and large, or at least our lack of failures, can be more or less correlated with our capacity to deceive: A playing up of one's qualities here; a cover up of one's misdemeanours there. O'Brien knew that better than any – Brandwood had seen him at parties with his piggy little snout in the trough, all chalky. Networking, is what the media types called it. His father had written for the Telegraph and been exactly the same. Courvoisier and call girls came to mind. Christ, he'd heard it on good authority that O'Brien himself was adopted! Daddy was a Jaffa, so the story went. Secrets were a part of Toby Boy's inheritance, just as they were for each of us.

But the pretence of innocence, the hypocrisy of it, that was the thing. It was supercharged. The old school understated 'tut-tut, well, let's get on with business' was just not enough anymore, apparently. O'Brien and his ilk, these mewing, midday Milquetoast types, had brought into fashion a public hand-wringing that made Brandwood's skin crawl. Weeping and wailing via their multitudinous media platforms about this injustice or that iniquity then pocketing their pay-checks and sending little Toby to the same alma mater that 'so looked after' him and papa. They didn't even have the balls, like his own cretinous son, to actually stand for anything. Go out and chain yourself to something, Mr O'Brien, if you're so horrified and concerned. But no. The moral was not the point – the *appearing to care* about the moral was far more important. Image was everything. And it was the same with this fucking inquiry. People who had been happy to let sleeping dogs lie for nearly three decades suddenly digging around in the dirt like what was left of their sorry little lives depended on it. What exactly happened at the briefing, Mr James? Wasn't it clear what was intended for the region all along, Mr James? Well – whatever fucking happened to bowing-out gracefully? Whatever fucking happened to fucking decorum?

Brandwood's face had started to rouge in the back of Japhet's wonderfully maintained cab, seething at the sheer insubordination he'd been subjected to, but his steadily brewing outrage was at least delivering some physical benefit. As his nasty fantasies started to run away with him, he was transported back to the sweaty embrace of the Somerset Room, where Dame Williamson was pursing her wrinkled lips around a request for his final comments and Brandwood felt himself rising heroically, unbuckling the restrictive nuisance of his oddly tailored trousers and striding towards the honourable lady, hips level with her chairbound facial orifices, to issue the most glorious Bismarcking ever witnessed within the walls of the Royal Palace. And just like that, he was there: Tesco Express and fully erect.

***

Brandwood crept wearily through the front door of his Richmond home at ten minutes past four in the morning, stopping on the edge of their hall-length paisley rug, where he removed his brogues, an action long automatised by guilt. He put one arm against the wall for support. The other hung wearily from his shoulder like a rag. He could barely muster the strength to take off his coat. Checking for any tell-tale residuals on his person, padding and patting himself down like his own jaded, one-armed prison guard, he sighed, hooked his mac over a radiator and shuffled further into the darkened hallway.

He sniffed the air. It was ribboned with the maudlin scent of open alcohol containers and the other tell-tale signs of his son's presence were in attendance too. There was a spilled pouch of tobacco on the sideboard and items of clothing, his jacket, his sweater, were dropped at intervals down the hallway. Brandwood put his keys down gently on top of the still unopened letter from his doctor and shuffled sock-hushed down the hall towards the large sitting room-cum-kitchen where he fully expected to find Milo passed out somewhere. Sure enough, his oafish offspring was stripped to the waist and splayed grotesquely over their petrol blue velvet sofa, completely unconscious and proudly displaying his bulging gut above a pair of recently pissed skinny jeans.

Though it rankled, Brandwood could not leave his son in such a state. There were only so many times a housekeeper could encounter such ruination before one had to issue a raise or have them replaced. Brandwood liked the current one, though he couldn't for the life of him remember her name. Pegita, was it? Surely not. So, he set about peeling the soggy denim from around Milo's legs before straightening him up a little and throwing a cashmere blanket over the length of his bulky frame. In all of this upheaval, Milo's expression did not change one jot. Eyes shut, slack jawed, he gawked blindly at whatever private, booze-addled visions were painted on the backs of his eyelids. Brandwood brushed the hair from his son's round face and looked at those closed eyes. They were Elizabeth's eyes, with her same beautiful, dark lashes. He wondered if there was any way to make any of it, this almighty mess he´d fashioned for himself, halfway right. His wife was lying alone upstairs. He could go and lie down next to her and confess all, purge himself, receive absolution. He could be pretty sure Elizabeth would not leave him. It was probably time to get out of the service anyway. Or nothing so dramatic, even. He could have just gone up and lay there a while, silently, sharing the same space for a few minutes, man and wife. But he didn't.

Open on the coffee table next to Milo was a half-drunk bottle of brandy, Brandwood's best, which he scooped up now and replaced in the cabinet, but not before pouring himself a decent measure. He carried the glass to the bay window to look out upon the naked desirability of the deserted street where they'd lived for twenty years. His street. Home. Save for the sodden, heaving breaths of his sleeping man-child, the scene was wonderfully quiet and still. Elizabeth was upstairs. The letter was on the sideboard. He took a sip of his drink and closed his eyes. He wanted to properly taste the expensive liquor in his mouth but, finding no flavour he could put a name to, he opened his eyes again and sighed. Outside, not even a leaf moved in the hedgerows. There was no one watching now, no one but him. No cat, no creature of any kind, skulked or stirred to sully the picture. There was just his own dark shape, silhouetted against the proud, enduring symmetry of Georgian architecture in the blue light of an approaching dawn.

Alte Oper

'DEM WAHREN SCHOENEN GUTEN.'
('To the true, the beautiful, the good.' *Inscription
on the frieze at the Alte Oper, Frankfurt.*)

*My name, since you did not ask, is Lubo. It does not matter to
you, I know. God bless, I not offend. You like my coat? It is good
coat. God bless it and you and me. God bless us all that walk these
golden streets, these painted squares. God bless your coin, your
briefcase, your job, your click, click heels to the U-Bahn train.
God bless my hands, my strong hairline, my tower of plastic cups,
my Samsung Galaxy J5 phone with crack screen but is still good.
You see nothing of me matters much to you, or to anyone. God
bless and thank you, I mean no harm. I super honest. Not like the
Sinti. Phwah! I spit. You wise man, wise lady. You know difference.
And since you are wise, you know that nothing ever matters much
at all. You've already worked that out, yes, nothing matters. Not
down here. Not up there. You see (you must), God bless, God
willing – your life, up there, filled like your pockets (they're good
pockets, hand stitched) with gold and silver words and shiny ideas
and hopes, it is only really stink-shit, the glittery piss of a lazy God,
like me, like mine, like Lubo, in the end.*

But if you met me in the street you would not think that. Oh God, Christ and his many anointed saints – no! Oh no oh no oh no. Holding your breath you would either bless yourself without waiting for God, making the cross real quick like Jesus freak in big Dom church, or maybe you would think nothing in your fat, important head if you met me, saw me, if we met. God bless you. God bless us both. If you met me in the street, you would likely not even look down at me – I'm down here, twit twoo, I wear this strong coat from army – and in not looking you would be judge of yourself much better, much more. God knows, he always knew, you would walk right past and quick too. Straight past my tower. Trot trot, there but for the grace of… By God, though, if – only if – you did look at me, if you stopped to put for me a few cents in my cups or hand me that coffee you are carrying so quickly between the places you must go, you would not understand me and I would not understand you. No no no. No way.

It is, most of all, a language thing. I have little that you'd know. What I have, is from a place you'd think of as Eastern Europe, loosely, just like that, without having any shitting sense of where or what I mean, or lives of people they live there, imagining mostly things that are wrong. It is not Europe where I am from. It is entirely different continent. No, the only understanding between you and me would be dumb. Our contract silent, grubby, the old one that was always there but never written. The one between the needy and the rich: that I will beg money of you, and you may decide to give it. But even a man like me, like Lubo, God bless him, has a story to tell. This ring, in my hands, my good hands that God has blessed, has a story all of its own. And as long as I have it and your attention, by God in Heaven who barely looks our way anymore, I am going to tell it.

This place, Opern Platz by the Alter Oper, this is my home. My little country, all on his own, away from them bad Arabs of Kaiserstrasse, those nasty Romanians too, the miserable Sinti, who get everywhere, God curse them and all their endless families. God curse them with the winds that whip this square, the snow you like to think so magical. This here is mine with my phone, my good hair line, my strong coat and hands. This I have. It has everything I need. Thick bushes, big bins, serious arches. Yes, my country, like old country, is rich and it stretches here across the road to the hot vents of the UPS towers on Bockenheimer. All around the perimeters of Rothschildpark it stretches, along Reuterweg, up and down the length of Grunerbergweg, but not as far as the park there, too many rich people and their police are there, back down Oederweg and through the green bushy Stadtrand of Bockenheimer anlage with all the diseased and blind fucking rabbits – coochy-coo, mixy-moo – until you get back here. I don't go down in U-Bahn station or S-Bahn stop of Taunus Anlage. Dirty places. Hardly ever do I go where I am heading now, to the Bahnhofsviertel, gods above and devils below us. You'll find out about those places. They are in in the story, not you worry.

And though I have never been inside the big, beautiful opera house that I say now my home, this story is kind of opera too. About, maybe by, or even, for, a ring – which some have tried before – much grander, but not like this. And I know how each song goes just by being here. I am witness to these streets. The songs here are sung from between the bars, grills and gutters. They rattle on all our hacking coughs. Some parts of it I watched with my own eyes, heard with my own good ears, some of it is just in me. Inside. Don't even know how it got there. The knowledge of these things, it unfolds, like the meaning of the burning words in those infectious Italian lady songs, drifting from a gap in the big back doors like smoke, it works itself in, like cold and the dirt from the streets. But the operas we sing aren't so romantic. God bless us, our strong coats, our dark hearts. They are different, darker, all the different shades of black that you find in alley after midnight. They might start and end in a whorehouse. That is normal. You'll see.

You see, you know me, by now, my name is Lubo, nice to meet, but that good little good boy man who has just dropped this ring

in my hand, accidentally (must to say), is name Marcel. And he
has been hanging around Haus 69 am Bahnhof far too much for
a good-boy man. He has lost something. Something very old and
valuable to him. And by rubbing it just so, I can make it sing and
tell you all the stories I already know by simple of my always being
here. So, now, you listen to Lubo. Let us hear the song a ring can
sing.

Marcel

Marcel Kleemeyer sat at the end of the prostitute´s bed and
turned his precious inheritance nervously around the properly
appointed finger. He was not in any way sure, as he had been just
moments ago, swaying violently in the street, of the logic that
had brought him so decidedly to this place. He had been trying
his best to listen to the ring, just as his beloved grandmother had
always counselled, and it had told him to fuck a prostitute.

Oma's ring had been quite clear on this. It had argued, with
some persuasiveness, through a series of strong discussions
and frank vodkas along a sleazy stretch of Kaiserstrasse's
schmutziest bars, that the most sensible way to allay the sexual
insecurity slowly blighting his long and loving relationship with
the woman he hoped to marry, was to have sex with another
woman, a stranger, for cash. That way, he might prove his
redblooded manhood to, well, himself and bury once and for all
the naggingly persistent suspicion that he might, in fact, be…
Well, suddenly, that idea seemed absurd and the ring, despite
his nervous fretting, was now annoyingly silent on the matter.

Turning the centuries-old band of dull gold and glinting
rubies around the slight circumference of his slender digit, the
cloying scent of perfume swimming greasily in the back of his
throat and curdling behind his eyes, Marcel sought to work up
the bravery to look the undeniably beautiful woman behind
him, Ruby, as she called herself, square in the face… or even
square in the tits. He could focus on her round, sexy tits, that

would be the thing. It was even encouraged, here, surely, whilst simultaneously seeking to fight down the impulse to vomit all over the plush, rouge carpet of her purple-lit boudoir. The flashing of blue neon blinked through the net curtains of the one small rectangular window. The room seemed unbearably close and warm. Panic, confusion and nausea wrestled each other through a bewildering fug of overstimulation. None of which, understandably, had made his cock go hard.

"I'm sorry about this," said Marcel, more than a little pathetically, "I don't usually…"

Ruby, as Rahel had allowed herself to be called in the two years since she had arrived at Haus 69, had seen it many times before. The heavily liquored impulse fuck comprised more than half of her nightly business here, ensconced as she was within a web of dive bars and strip clubs in Frankfurt's notorious Bahnhofsviertel, and had the double-edge benefit that she was often required to do little more than stroke a sheepishly flaccid cock for a few moments before the sorry score chucked his supper on the shagpile and was ejected by security. The smell was the obvious and pervasive draw back. The stink of alcohol and vomit had come to be as familiar to her as her own sweat, along with the many other secretions that were serviced in her tiny, expensively rented room. It was this fact that accounted for the overwhelming odour of perfume, not whorish extravagance, as so many punters falsely assumed. Human sick needs some strong scents to overpower it, but for her, such concerns were secondary. The important thing, rule number one, regardless of how it all played out, was to get the cash in your strongbox early.

"It's okay," she said automatically, reaching around Marcel and starting to unbuckle his belt with detached intimacy, whilst feeling with the other hand for the profile of a wallet. "It's all okay. Come here…"

As she pawed around Marcel's taut waist, looking over his shoulder, Ruby caught a glimpse of the object of his undivided attention and was immediately triggered. She saw herself as a child, sitting cross-legged, thumbing through a jeweller's catalogue in a bare, uncarpeted room. Rubies were, as her working name attested, her very favourite of all her desired gemstones. They enchanted her in a way that wasn't healthy. Her inveterate mother had promised her one, just one, when she passed her *Abitur* exams, but Rahel had not stuck around in Hamburg long enough to be disappointed again. No promise was worth that amount of misery. This ring, Marcel's, which boasted five rubies in total – two small pairs positioned either side the large central stone – was easily the most beautiful she had ever seen in the wild. It sang to her immediately, in a voice she almost recognised, to a melody she thought she knew. She put her powdered cheek to the nape of Marcel's neck and whispered,

"Well, isn't that lovely? Who's it for?" Meaning: to me, to me, give the ring to me. Clients were prone to impulsive acts when they arrived as soused as Marcel clearly was, and she'd received similar tokens, though never quite as beguiling as this one, before. She didn't care to think how many girlfriends, fiancées, mistresses and wives she'd deprived of their full romantic climax and momentary hypertelial happiness. But fuck 'em. This was her world and here the arts of suggestion and seduction worked hand in hand. Whatever advantage you might have, including some poor John's drunken disorientation, press it. Crush it, in fact. Take them for everything you could.

"It's my grandmother's…" said Marcel, not answering the question. From a room above, the timbered thump of bodily collision reverberated through the wall and mixed with the pounding bass of the club below. In some of those other rooms grown men were being whipped and beaten, they were having their winkies swaddled like babies, arseholes were being tongued, some arseholes were doing the tonguing, they were ejaculating on and into perfect strangers, but there was nothing so despicably fascinating to Ruby as what was unfolding here. She wrapped herself a little more tightly around Marcel's midriff, pressing her body against his back, as her small room seemed suddenly to separate from the rest of the house, isolated garishly, a soft warm pod of purple light and synthetic tenderness within a heaving sprawl of coarse desire.

Stop a moment and step back. Retreat a little from the brash chamber of this one room, drifting backward at an even pace, the action frozen, and you would see a network of others, looking more or less the same, hive-like, in the brothel next door, then repeated again, a matrix of degeneracy, in the one right next to that. Allow yourself to drift back further and you would see a uniform grid of electrified, criss-crossing streets with their glowing lights – Frankfurt's Bahnhofsviertel- the grand old central station squatting proudly at its centre, a black toad on a gaudy lily. Float still further into the distant cloudless night and see the bunched, viral patches of the phosphorescent cities, their luminous, land-spanning tendrils binding Germany to Europe, Europe to Asia, all the continents together on this blinking, spinning half-dark globe. And from such a vantage as our lonely moon, looking down on this blue dot, you might conclude, as a privileged few have, well, what does any of it matter? But from where Ruby is sitting, the whole spinning mess matters very much indeed. Ruby has a singular focus. Which is all a person really needs. And hers is no wider than a finger's width. So as Marcel sits, rigid in her embrace, still turning the ring to some inexplicable, universal frequency, Ruby continues, delicately, to unbutton his fly. She is as transfixed as he is, both locked into the moment. She nestles her face close to his, feels the wiry scuff of his four-day stubble, and kisses him softly. He barely flinches, but she senses something moving. In him. Inside. Their chests heave together. Their breathing starts to synchronise. She pushes a hand down into the dark thatch of his pubic hair and exhales the words "It's beautiful..." hotly into his ear. And that is what breaks the spell.

Marcel pulled himself away, suddenly, to the furthermost corner of the bed and sat, hunched awkwardly, facing the door.

"I'm sorry," he mumbled again, as Ruby fell forward, before righting herself. She sat up sharply, embarrassed and irritated, then remembered where she was.

"Yeah, well, it's one hundred euros for one hour. I need the cash now." Ruby said, sniffing, then propping herself on one arm.

She watched then as this oddly handsome oddball fished in his pocket and slapped the cash, a single crisp green note, onto the mattress without looking round. He'd clearly come prepared, which made her wonder. She snatched up the note quickly and deposited it in a small, lockable chest in her bedside drawer. She stood in her high heels looking down at the unusual stranger, her long, pale slender limbs, her sleek blonde hair, the small sensual paunch of her supple belly all framed in the opalescent light, quite divinely ignored. She felt a mixture of relief, incredulity and disgust. He cut such a strange figure, even without the rare antique he fingered so insistently. His shoulder length hair was scooped back into a greasy pony. His olive complexion was darkened with thick brown eyebrows, a short scruffy beard and long, beautiful eyelashes that flickered over his haunted hazel eyes. He was a good-looking man, athletic too, and in another state, he might have been what she'd come to consider as bonus work, a *gimme*, a fairly painless undertaking. But not like this. It felt strange. She shook her head and sat down on the bed again.

With the money safe, Ruby relaxed slightly, though she knew from experience how important it was to remain vigilant. Strange Johns like this one could go from timid little bedwetters to wild-eyed chokers in a heartbeat, given a certain unknown quantity, so she kept her distance and sat with her back against the plush red headboard of her bed, her knees drawn up, but casually, as though she were chatting with a college dormmate in the university she never did attend. She asked, softly, if there was anything she could do for him. He seemed very sad and it was his money after all. If he wanted to talk, they could talk.

"I'm supposed to give this ring to the woman I will marry," said Marcel, instantly, tears in his voice, sounding exactly like the thing that he was: something trapped. "My Oma said I'd know... the ring, if you get me, would let me know. When I'd found the right girl. You know. The right... girl." He stopped as his voice buckled. Ruby buckled a little with him.

"Oh, Schatzy. I see..." she said, using her real voice for an unguarded moment. Something in his hunched uncertainty, the desperate trembling of his shoulders, the dreadful distance behind his brown eyes told her everything she needed to know. She understood. She felt a swell of human empathy for the lonely creature perched on the end of her bed, compounded by the certain knowledge that there really was nothing *she* could do for him. She composed herself and let Ruby take over again. There was still an advantage to be pressed.

"So, listen, it could be that thing is just weighing you down, right?" She offered, breezily. She could sense that the situation was sobering him, so it was best to act fast. "You can't go carrying Grandma round in your pocket all your life, can you? I could help you get rid of it, if you want? I know some people." She thought of Ibra. Immediately, she thought of him. Coiled.

"Oh God, no, I could never..." he said, then hesitated. "My Oma... she got this ring from her Tante. Her Tante gave it to her, before she went, before they all went, to... Theresienstadt, if you get me."

"Sure. I get you," said Ruby, firmly, though she felt Rahel wavering in the notes of sadness she couldn't hide. She shut her out again and pressed on.

"So, what is it then? You've found a girl? Or a guy? But you can't go through with it?"

"Sophia," he said. Each syllable ached.

Sophia was the girl to whom he would be married. He still believed, or at least hoped, that this was true. He had decided it with certainty more times than he could remember. Or the ring had decided it for him. It assured him that she was the one.

Sophia was the most wonderful woman, after his own grandmother, that Marcel had ever met. She was a year older than him, at thirty three, but still possessed the build and movements of a ballerina. Light as a leaf, she pirouetted from one moment to the next, her rich auburn hair always smelling like raspberries, fresh ones, on a light spring breeze. She wore men's cardigans several sizes too big for her at more or less any time of year. When she entered a room where people had gathered, she pulled a net of golden warmth over it, so that everyone felt suddenly better about wherever it was they were at. She was spellbinding.

Marcel and Sophia – they were known to most as a pair – met in university, at a party, like you are supposed to. They had been *just* friends for a whole term until that sacred day of drinking vodka from a hip flask and riding the Pater Noster at IG Farben Haus, before ending up in Marcel's messy room in his shared flat, where he had been delighted to discover just how much she excited him. Her small breasts. Her lithe, feline hips. She fascinated him and felt like relief. A relief from himself.

Bumbling from one semester to the next, they had helped each other negotiate the vagaries of their Art History degrees. Sometimes floundering, sometimes basking in their shared sense of aimlessness, they questioned what it even was to have ambition in such a misdirected world and had been so completely a pair of arty pricks that, at times, they even annoyed themselves, but then laughed about that too, together. They read their favourite poems to each other and stopped in disbelief when they found themselves moved by the same lines, in the just the same way, more times that could, surely, have been chance.

One bright day, stretched out on the lush grass of the Grunerberg park, Sophia had summed up what it was they had together when she had turned to Marcel and told him, frankly,

"You give me permission just to be".

They had promised then that, whatever happened, they would help each other achieve their dreams in life – because that, more than sex, more than the rawness of fleeting passion – was what it truly meant to be partners.

It was Marcel, or more specifically his mother, who helped to finance Sophia's transfer on to a Masters in Sustainable Development when she had finally worked out what it was she really wanted to be doing. And it was Sophia, in turn, through her work for an international cosmetics firm, who had supported Marcel and his mother in the recent lean years, as their real estate business lurched from loss to loss, the fallout of years of poor planning and a deteriorating, dilapidated portfolio.

And everyone adored Sophia. Merle, his mother, especially. Their bond was such that it even seemed to compensate his lack of closeness with the woman who had helped to raise him, because the bulk of that job had been done by his Oma. Marcel's father, the heir to a large amount of property in Frankfurt and beyond, had died when he was only six years old. The business had therefore passed into the hands of his mother, who had poured the dark energy of her grief into ensuring its survival. She had succeeded, barely, but at some cost to the relationship with her son. It meant that Marcel's Oma, the wise old woman who had survived a genocide without sacrificing a shred of her humanity, became his everything.

But Oma had never met Sophia. In a way he thought of as fated, she had died during his first week of university, shortly before he and Sophia met. This had played its part in the attraction. Marcel, exposed and grieving, had seemed so much more real to Sophia than the plastic millennial hippies that floated about the university campus taking selfies of themselves making peace signs. For his part, Sophia seemed to carry something of his Oma's spirit. That radiance of compassion. That effortless ability to soothe. And, of course, there was the ring. The last thing his grandmother had given to him, her last words, in fact:

"Find her, Mauschen. The ring will let you know."

It might be deemed unwise to place such heed in the drug-addled utterances of a dying pensioner, but whatever the concoction of hormones, fate and circumstance, Marcel and Sophia had been inseparable since the day they'd met. If there were such a thing as 'the one', then surely she was it. If it wasn't for one unalterable human fact: Simon.

Simon Gravenreuth had been a friend since childhood and had, briefly, worked for his mother's firm too. Brash, confident and an utterly irredeemable cunt, he had been in equal parts as perfect for the world of property rental as he was cast in the role of unattainable object of erotic fantasy, a part which he had occupied for a far longer stretch in Marcel's imagination.

The entirely one-sided obsession had developed in their teenage years, when Simon flitted tantalisingly in and out of Marcel's life as the son of one of Merle's wealthier clients. They had been to primary school together, but nothing had stirred, then Simon swept back into frame as a muscular 14-year-old rowing champion, a mane of parted golden hair and the jawline of Nazi propagandists' dreams. Something in Marcel was woken.

During the hot summer of 2003, in which Merle sold Simon's mother a farmhouse in the Hessich countryside – Oberquembach, a place forever fixed in Marcel's imagination – they saw each other every few days, becoming cautiously closer and closer. The women, both rich and husbandless in any real sense – Simon's father was a charming but often drunk philanderer – were each seeking to school their sons in the art of the deal, with the eventual aim being their progenies' smooth transition into the positions of wealth and power to which they were surely destined. Only one of them would make it, as it turned out – and Simon made the running early. He played the prodigious son brilliantly, offering pithy observations and asking pertinent questions about development potential, whilst making faces behind his mother's back and sharing pornographic images with Marcel on his state-of-the-art Nokia. Marcel was bewildered by him. He was aroused and confused by what they looked at together. It was not so much the images. They were so graphic as to seem somehow absurd. It was the closeness that Marcel found exciting.

Then, one warm midsummer's afternoon as the women signed contracts, wore summer hats and drank champagne in the farmhouse courtyard, Simon challenged Marcel to a test of strength in the field that adjoined the property: a wrestling match. A bloody wrestling match! The first one to pin the other to the ground wins. Pin. The. Other. To. The. Ground. Marcel's head could have popped.

Simon had taken off his sky-blue Ralph Lauren polo shirt before waiting for an answer. At the merest glimpse of his smooth broad chest framed in the blazing sun Marcel had to forcefully stifle an erection. Gathering himself and his cock, which he flattened against his belly and trapped under the elastic of his bright yellow board shorts, Marcel sheepishly agreed. He didn't know what else to do. Simon had so much more conviction than he possessed himself in just about everything they did. It was the end of the deal on the house, nearing the end of the summer, and maybe a last chance of sorts. Marcel suddenly felt a strange symbiosis with his pulsing member that he had not known before; both of them were trapped but utterly, ecstatically compelled.

Marcel refused to remove his own T-shirt. He couldn't risk it. For a start, he had the head of his penis poking up above the drawstring of his shorts like a veiny, pink hatted soldier in a laughable, daisy-lined trench. But more than that, he knew suddenly that if he took off one garment, he would want to remove them all, and all of Simon's, too: he would want not to take them off, but rip them, clawing at them, tearing, discarding them in an ecstasy of clotheslessness; to leave them both panting, hard and naked, with a fucking match or a fight to the death the only conceivable conclusions. No, he tried to focus on the task in hand: wrestling just competently enough to allow Simon to pin him, but quickly, and without shame to either party. That he could do. He waited agonisingly as Simon unnecessarily stamped out the outline of a ring in the knee-length grass, ludicrously spat on his hands, and approached, crouching.

It was all over before it had started. Simon pinned Marcel in a matter of seconds. Marcel felt the snaring of an ankle, a sudden impact to his shoulder and he was rushing backwards into the lush green grass, the blue skies yawning above him, dreamily, then replaced in seconds by the wide, sneering face of his boy conqueror. Marcel couldn't have resisted even if he'd wanted to, so much bigger and stronger was his friend. But he hadn't wanted to. Being beneath Simon, with Simon shirtless and grinning, was exactly where he wanted to be. It was the purest expression of desire that he had ever known. "Forget the heart," he thought, "it is the cock, most of all, that wants what it wants." Marcel worked hard to ensure that Simon stayed squatted on his chest and didn't straddle him any lower, to avoid the sure and certain contact of stiffy and arse, along with the dreadful, unchartered upshot that would surely follow. He managed it, despite himself, but from that moment on, Marcel's body had lusted, with every thread and fleck of pulsing tissue in it, to bind itself to Simon's. It wanted to be near him, underneath him, inside him if it could. But he only felt that ache for Simon. No one else, man or woman, had the same effect. Not even Sophia, the girl the ring so clearly said he should marry. Marcel stopped talking and his head sagged lower still.

"Kraaaaaasss." Ruby said, engrossed in the story and by now lying on her side, one hand tucked between her knees, the other propping her chin, the way she'd listened to her mother's sometimes sad, sometimes hilarious late-night train-wreck reportage. She had almost, but not entirely, forgotten about the ticking of the clock.

Rahel

'Life in plastic, it's fantastic…hmmm, hmmm, hmmm, yeah.'

In the big exam hall of the Alfred Doblin Gymnasium, Bergdorf, Rahel Dest watched the second hand of the huge, Bahnhof style clock tick painfully overhead and she hummed, impatiently. She thought about Alexanderplatz, Berlin. Not Berlin, Alexanderplatz. She had just given the last of whatever time and energy she had left for the novel by old Alfie D writing an excellent essay – grade one, she felt sure – that she'd trotted out in double quick time to the sour-faced consternation of her miserable, on-looking German teacher, Frau Blinder. No, she was thinking of the place. The real, tourist-ridden, shop-laden, history soaked, chemically assisted, consumer culture Mecca that old Alfred had sought to freeze in time almost a century prior, but that had gone on grimly with and without him, through wars, walls and webinars, chalking off the years like a prisoner of conscience, counting the very days until the moment of Rahel's own inimitable arrival.

This was it. These exams, their end measured out by the ticking of this big dumb clock, were the start of something huge. In a matter of months, before she even received the results she had punished herself for – as they were a stone cold certainty – she would jump on a train to the German capital with a suitcase of luggage, directions to the Literature Dept. of Humboldt University in hand, and she would not look back. The last thing she would need from her mother, the very last thing she would ask of her, would be the small endowment she had waiting for her from her absent father's decade of alimony payments. That would see her through the first few months of accommodation, course expenses and administration fees. She was prepared, happy even, to work for the rest.

She gnawed on a stubby, raw thumbnail and waited. She twisted a sleek, auburn lock of hair around her index finger. Light from the high windows of the gymnasium captured columns of shimmering dust suspended before the heavy double doors that marked the boundary between this world and the next. Out there was everything she had waited for. The sounds of twitching papers rustled behind her and she felt the sudden, flicked impact of something tiny strike her calf. She looked behind and saw her friend Nele grinning, eyes motioning furtively to the floor below. Rahel leaned down, one eye fixed on the back of the prowling Blinder, then picked up the pea ball note of crumpled paper. She silently unravelled it beneath the lip of her desk and read the words:

HERE. WE. GO!

Rahel's heart sang. It was a song of beginnings and of endings too. The beginnings in wait were so rapturously wonderful that she could have opened her mouth and the let the rising high notes carry her all the way to her new life right there and then, straight to that better place, the capital, with nicer people and, most of all, the promise of a fair fucking chance.

'Come on Barbie, let's go party…'

But the other song, the song of endings, was the one she had rehearsed for longer. This song was made of broken promises and the limp, wheezing expiration of hope. It was made of lies and filthy looks from men she barely knew in dirty rooms she was supposed to call home. It was composed of tears on forgotten birthdays, stains on sheets, broken needles, hidden bottles, roaming hands, midnight escapes and the days and days spent waiting for the noise of a key in the door. It was sung in her own voice but it was written by her mother, and at eighteen, she had already waited too long to be done singing it.

On the journey home from school, the last time she would make it, Rahel rehearsed the words she needed one more time, so that she would have the strength to break herself free from the person she loved and hated, in equal measure, most in the world. She would be gracious. She would be kind. She would not stoop to her mother's level. She would ask for what she was due, leave what little she could afford, and get out of town as soon as it could all be settled.

She felt sure that she could do it and yet, with all that preparation, with a lifetime of rehearsal, that her goodbye performance should still go so spectacularly wrong was, even years after the disaster, something of a surprise. When she looks back on it later, sifting the debris, as she is bound to do, over and over, it is almost as if she herself were not directly involved. She watches it back, watches herself stroll right into it, the disaster, from outside the event. Looking down on herself and her mother in that tiny flat, the picture blurry, dazed and bewildering, hearing the shrieking and the screaming in dull, distant echoes, is something like watching an attack of frenzied sharks as they tear each other to pieces inside a reinforced tank. She sees flashes of body parts, streaks of black mascara, red scratches and puffy eyes, the flat register of a slap, the strangely still and precise crookedness of a picture on the wall, a scented candle being placed inexplicably in a brown handbag, the crunching of glass underfoot, and finally, a woman she feels she hardly knows and is sure she will never see again, screaming, receding into the distance, getting smaller and smaller.

'I'm a Barbie girl, in a Barbie world...'

There had been no money put away. There were no rubies in wait, no pot of jewels, no reward of any kind. There was just one final crushing-but-predictable disappointment and an awful reckoning that had been building for years. She remembers walking from the scene, her sad and hasty collection of bags bumping against her legs, humming *Barbie Girl* by Aqua to fill the space in her head where the thoughts wanted to crowd, raw and jostling, wringing their hands and sobbing. She walked and walked. She hummed *Barbie Girl*. The bags banged against her pale calves and kept a rhythm. Walk. Walk. Walk a deliberate walk. She had no sense of where she was headed, but a part of her knew exactly where she would end up. When she finally came to her senses, when the humming stopped, she was standing, rain streaked, in the middle of a famous street, in the seediest but most familiar part of town. Sure enough, she'd arrived at the only place her desperation knew to take her, staring blankly up at the flashing neon sign outside a club in Hamburg's Rieperbahn. *SEX* is what the sign said. Over and over. On repeat.

Since that day, Rahel, even after her transformation into the peroxide blond Ruby, hummed to distract herself. When she started, that very next day, letting herself be fucked for money, figuring that she might as well get paid for something that was already happening anyway, she hummed to block out the feelings. She hummed to block out thoughts, especially the repeating one that told her any one of those men inside her could be her mother's new squeeze, or worse: any one of those men could be her father. And, of course, the customers complained about the humming. It was off-putting, they said. So, Ruby tried doing it in her head, but it wasn't enough. She knew she had to get away. She had to get out of Hamburg.

'You can brush my hair, undress me everywhere…'

It was still Rahel's plan, eventually, to go to Berlin. It was still Rahel's plan, for a long while at least, to go to university. But in between, Ruby needed to make money, and somewhere other than that north coast Hansestadt, with its constant reminders of Mutti and the father who never was. So, she accepted the help of her newly found pimp-cum-confident, Rudi – who said he knew a guy who ran a sound little operation down in Frankfurt, where all the girls were looked after, and everything was done right. Rooms were affordable, the security was solid. He could even sort the train fare, he said, if she made sure to mention his name. That place was Haus 69. Six years later, she was still there, hearing the heartfelt confession of a tortured soul much like herself, tracing his sordid, well-worn lines of human misery to their all too obvious source, aching with the sympathy of the attuned confidante, whilst covertly typing out a text message to the one man, if you could even call him that, who might finally deliver what she'd been promised long ago.

Ibra

Ibra was not the manager of Haus 69. Far from it. In fact, Ibra was sneered at and reviled by brothel owners throughout Frankfurt's red-light district and beyond for being just the kind of low-life opportunist who gave their law-abiding trade a bad name. Not that he cared. He was a specialist and proud of it. Ibra did not need to own a brothel of his own, because his sphere of influence was the street. He owned the streets. All of them. Through his begging gangs, his forlornly willing boys and girls that trawled the city at night on his behalf, he could be everywhere at once. Wherever need, greed or desperation had undone someone – there he was. Johnny on the spot.

Ibra specialised in manipulating, extorting and often outright robbing street Johns who strayed away from the relative safety and order of the whorehouses in the police monitored Bahnhofsviertel. His centre of operation was the stinking men's toilet block at the Alte Oper U-Bahn stop. This was a well-known cottaging location, so Ibra had a number of dummy swordsmen working the square, the lifts and stairs, reporting directly to him. Their job was to tempt in unsuspecting victims for some nameless, stringless, trouserless fun and then fleece them for everything they had by the urinals.

The usual trick was for the bait to lead the John inside the toilet block and wait until his exposed member was in his hand. At this point, Ibra or a similarly appointed heavy would step from a cubicle and take a snap of said member with a smart phone. At the same time, the bait himself would pull a knife and explain the new and seriously deflating terms of negotiation to the hapless stooge. The combination of shame, documentary evidence and threat of serious violence was enough to compel most gents to give up whichever precious items it was in their power to relinquish, including large amounts of cash, so it had become a fairly reliable source of income for the unscrupulous snake's head.

But Ibra was an enterprising man in the true spirit of his times. As well as this racket, he also organised a begging gang of indentured homeless slaves that stretched the length and breadth of Frankfurt city centre, their cardboard *Bitte, 1 euro, essen* signs almost as ubiquitous a trademark as MacDonald's golden arches that Ibra so idolised, along with a sideline in street sex and security for working girls who wanted to make extra cash, off the books of their Bordello bosses. And this was how he'd found Ruby.

Ibra looked down at his phone to check the time. 22:50. The Friday night show at the old opera house would be closing soon. *Das Ring des Nebelungen – Wagner*. What delighted Ibra more than anything in his job was picking off marks from the abundant ranks of the upper classes who frequented that grand old building. A typical opera crowd made the most wonderful poaching ground. In less than ten minutes, the ornate doors of one of Frankfurt's most treasured icons would disgorge, like a sluice gate, hundreds of stuffed shirts all starched by their own self-importance and supposed moral fibre. There was no better place for snaring the weak. Pumped full of ceremony, drunk on champagne, giddy on orchestral, homoerotic pomp – these toffs practically jumped into his net. Ibra and his boys did their best work on opera nights. The fishes he reeled in, slick with their own fat, never looked better than when flopping and gutted on the tiled floor of his shit-house stronghold, spilling their tears and their wallets among the excrement of the great un-hosed. There was a beauty in it. *To the true, the beautiful, the good.* "Yes," thought Ibra. "To us."

A thin, ironic smile striped itself across his face animating his dark, angular features against the indigo-ink sky. He looked out across the grand, bistro-lined plaza approvingly. He belonged here. He was a handsome man and rich, too. He was getting richer by the day. He straightened out his suit jacket and readied himself for action. He sucked hard on the Lucky Strike that he had perfected smoking in three long draws. He tried to be in the moment, to concentrate on this most enjoyable, most rewarding aspect of his work. But his mind remained on Ruby.

Ibra wanted Ruby badly. He had wanted her from the first moment he had seen her enter Haus 69, ducking past his little porchway posse of harlots and thieves to start her night's work, her pale skin and long blond hair shimmering in the blinking lights. He had never seen a girl like her before. But this attraction was more than sexual desire: He could fuck Ruby anytime he wanted to. He had done, in fact. And had the cash to do it again, many times over. But he knew that it was nothing more than a rental. Her body, rented to him, for one paltry hour or so. Ibra liked to own things. People included. People especially. When you own a thing, it is completely in your power. You can destroy it if you want to, because it's yours. You can use that thing in whichever way you want.

Ibra himself had only the vaguest sense where this possessive impulse came from, but he'd had it all his life. He guessed it was to do with dislocation – of having come from nothing. Ibra did not know which country he came from and he was not even sure of his second name. He could not remember his parents and had no recollection of ever having seen them in the flesh. Salihamodzic was the name he had taken from the street uncle who had groomed him and taught him his trade. It was the name he used for any legitimate business interests. But having nothing, no family, not even a past – this, he guessed, was what drove him to collect things. The more possessions he had, the more cars, the more jewellery, the more watches, wallets and phones, the more people; the more things he controlled, the more connected to the world he felt. And now, above all things, he wanted to have Ruby.

All of which made her cool disinterest in him even harder to bare. He was tortured by the thoughts of so many cocks inside her, defiling such a thing of beauty, without him gaining a single quantifiable thing from those transactions. Ruby knew her worth, knew that she was much more than street fuck, so Ibra needed something beyond the offer of perversity and danger money that usually brought the desperate girls to him. He felt certain he would find it, though: her weakness. People are always weak, in the end. When you have watched enough men follow a stranger into a filthy, dank room that smells like an open sewer, you come to see how our weaknesses almost always outweigh our strengths. People have buttons. Find the right button to push and people will do what you want them to do.

He felt sure he would find Ruby's. Something would happen to bring her to him. He was contemplating this, Ruby's lack of obvious buttons and his intrepid quest to find them, when something magical happened. Listening to the building crescendo of a Brahms concerto he played constantly on headphones just to intimidate associates, watching the wealthy, unsuspecting patrons pour from Alte Oper after another night of divine musical fantasy, whilst instinctively scouring the crowd for a face that reeked of weakness, he felt his phone vibrate and a short ping interrupt the unintelligible cacophony of classical violin assaulting his ears.

Incredibly, it was from her. With a single withering look, he delegated his peep show paparazzi role to an underling and peeled off from the crowd. Skirting the edge of Opern Platz, killing the volume on his mobile, he paced the short stretch of orange-lit parkway that led to Taunus Anlage, reading and rereading the message back to himself just to be certain.

"Sad fuck leaving Haus now. Long hair, stubble. Brown suede jacket. Direction Willy Brandt Platz. Has a ring. Get it and we talk."

Here, then, was the button. Ibra stowed the phone in his suit jacket and began the short sprint between the S-Bahn stop and the enormous, illuminated Euro sign at Willy Brand Platz in the middle of Frankfurt's banking district, his long limbs suddenly and unusually animated. His flat, polished shoes slapped the pavement with a clacking sound and he felt alive. He heard the wind whipping in his ears, the sharp, cool puffing of his own breath. He had not heard these sounds, the sounds of the chase, in years. People ran for him now. They scurried. They brought things to him. Things he desired. But this was his chance to pocket something so precious that he was prepared to do the leg work himself. The inner city air, with its petrochemical film of fumes from a thousand cars and air conditioning units, sweetly filled his lungs. His mind raced with all the ways he would use the thing he had coveted so long. He skidded into the square, stopped, and, panting, he surveyed the scene.

He saw nothing unusual. The flat, characterless expanse of concrete trapped between the towers was filled with the usual smattering of desperate beggars, some from his own crew, and weary, overworked bankers in dishevelled suits.

A woman in a layered head scarf, virtually bent double, shuffled up to him and pushed a *Bitte – 1 euro – Essen* sign under his nose, but when she looked up and saw his face she straightened with fear and pressed quickly on. Disgusted, Ibra wiped his hands on his suit jacket, pulled out a cigarette from the top pocket and lit it casually as he scanned the square. Through the silken threads of his own cigarette smoke, his eyes darted around the scene. He studied the criss-crossing gravel pathways that intersected the grassy park space at the foot of the grand, mirror clad Eurotower. He tracked the shifting movements by the dark fringes of trees and bushes. He was about to abandon the hunt, but then he saw what he was looking for: Hands stuffed in pockets, muttering to himself and staggering, Marcel weaved his way across the tram tracks right through the middle of the square in the direction of Hauptwache, the way that Ibra had just come. He exhaled a plume of smoke, crushed his cigarette under his heal and stepped out of the shadows.

Sad fuck was about right. The man before him was a mess and seemed genuinely troubled. He kept rubbing his face, stopping suddenly in the street, remonstrating angrily with no one in particular, then continuing his bedraggled shuffle. He looked unsure and unsteady. It might have been the simplest thing to merely walk straight up to the pathetic specimen and relieve him of his personal effects right there in the street, but Ibra preferred to employ more sophisticated methods, ones that involved less personal risk. Besides, he had not assembled such a fine collection of tools for no reason and like any master of his trade, he took great pleasure in selecting just the right tool for each specific job.

Following quietly, observing the mad, distracted chatter of his target as he wandered aimlessly towards a fate that Ibra himself would surely organise, he read with pleasure the sublime sadness in the creased, unkempt melancholy of his crinkled coat. Suddenly, he had a picture of the perfect complement to this lost and wandering soul – he pictured a butterfly wing, beautifully patterned but lifeless, crumpled and crushed in its own cocoon, broken before it could fly. He was already bringing up the name in his phone: Sajad.

Sajad

The night was warm and restful, but that did not matter. He was tired, but that did not mean a thing. Sajad had stopped expecting anything like luck, or rest, or mercy a long time since. He no longer searched for the hand of God in things, as he once had. *Khoda ruhyeaham raefteh.* What was the point?

There had been times on Sajad's journey – the long and testing road between continents – when he had thought he could detect a whisper. There were moments when he thought he could make out just the trace of a script. It was always hidden, obscured behind the cruel, relentless hardships of the living world, but he'd felt sure that it *was* there, hiding, somewhere. Once, clinging to the top of a sinking raft on a salt-lake between Iran and Turkey, Sajad had seen the full white moon reflected so perfectly in the distant, still waters that it seemed to him that all the heavens had been brought low, turned upside down and spread out upon the earth itself. Seeing them, those two moons, at the depth of his exhaustion, he had no longer cared if he lived or died. He stopped trying. He let the water take him, expecting to be swallowed up. Yet he had woken on the Turkish shore of Urmiya Gölü, Lake Urmia, broken and soaked... but whole. Alive.

He was certain then that this surrender had saved his life. God had spared him because he had given himself over to His will. But he has stopped looking for God on this forsaken continent. He only expects to be taught new indignities. In the hundreds of untracked days that Sajad had existed in Germany, for it could barely be called living, he had done so many unspeakable things that he couldn't bring himself to believe God was looking anymore. No God could even look upon the acts that occurred here, let alone want them done. He had taken men inside him, in his mouth, and elsewhere. He had hurt and been hurt, drawing blood, for other men to watch, for money. He had betrayed and been betrayed many times over; scraped his dinner from bins and gutters. He had taken food, God forgive him... he had taken food from children.

Tonight, the night was calm, but for a warm breeze. It was much like the one he remembered back in Kandahar; the way it whispered down the cobbled alleys, somehow finding its way here, onto the Fressgasse, where he had made his bed. He'd been there, in the doorway beneath a rusting scaffold, for three days. The summer had been exceptionally warm. The last few evenings he had avoided any incidents: no clashes with shop owners, no altercations with the growing number of other desperate men and women who shared the same streets. He had slept well, in fact. But still, he did not expect it to last. So, he was not at all surprised when he was summoned.

Sajad had been working for Ibra since he arrived in Frankfurt. The boss man who drove the big, cold lorry, the one that transported chilled meat and frozen people from Istanbul to Darmstadt, had delivered Sajad and the others directly to Ibra like so much cargo. They had filed out of the secret compartment, stinking and shaken, coated in their own waste and each other's and Ibra had lined them up and showed them a printed sheet, a bill, that listed the costs of their travel. He held it in front of their faces. The figures looked huge but were unintelligible. Not a single one of them had understood. The one thing they grasped, were made to grasp, was the sentence he had repeated, this businessman, this messiah in a suit, in Kurdish, in Arabic, in Persian Dari, his own dialect, in Urdu and Pashtoo and Punjabi and of course – the new holy tongue – English:

"You work for me now. You pay. One year. No choice. You leave, you finished."

That was two years ago. He'd heard no mention of the bill again since.

Most of the people Sajad had been shipped with, Afghans like him, he never saw again. He used to feel regret about that, but he felt very little anymore. They were sorted and sold that very day – many, it seemed, remained in Darmstadt. But Ibra took a liking to Sajad straight away. He had held him by the chin and whispered,

"Schoen, schoen, schoen," in his ear.

Sajad was a beautiful man. Dark skinned for his region, with thick black hair framing a slender, oval face – his unusual sapphire blue eyes possessed a depthless mystery which his soul found hard to match. People had always expected more from him than he felt able to give. His parents had such high hopes for him, the second youngest from three boys and four girls, that they had kept what little money they had for educating their children in reserve for him alone. His teachers, on the few occasions that schooling was possible or allowed, directed all their questions his way, though he had barely ever been able even to follow the lesson. When one night a band of rebels descended from the hills and took away his father, he had been expected to take the old man's place, though he was only thirteen. And it was this incommensurate expectation that had led him to make the trip to the Western promised land alone. His family simply expected him to make it. He didn't know how to disappoint them.

He thanked God, the threadbare, ragged bit that he still believed in, that they could not see where he had ended up. Sleeping in boxes. Begging for another man's gain. He picked up the phone and the small flick knife, both of which Ibra had given to him that first night in Frankfurt, and read with his broken German:

"U Bahn klo. Outside. Now. Cheeseburgers after. Macadonalds."

The toilet block of the Alte Oper U-Bahn stop was Sajad's own personal Hell. Pictures of it, the things that he had done there, came to him at night. He had a nightmare in which he watched himself, degraded like a dog, from the gap in the cubicle door. Trapped, his eye fixed to the repulsive sliver of black theatre that he couldn't un-see, he watched himself on all fours, hooded and gagged, always at the very periphery of his own vision, straining to see what he only wished he could shut out. He had to know. He had to know what they would make him do next.

But he never did know for sure. Because it was not enough for Ibra that Sajad should return there in his dreams. He sent them back down in reality, again and again, all of his boys – and Sajad, his prize possession – went most often. Down the steps they went, to make more trauma. To scar themselves and their victims. To build themselves a prison of thoughts, acts, images from which they would never be truly free. And afterwards, they ate cheeseburgers; the sick, paltry way that Ibra sealed his grubbiest deals.

Arriving at the U-Bahn steps, fists bunched, the knife stuffed into his ripped jeans pocket, he found Ibra lurking on the steps smirking, half in darkness, with a finger to his lips. There was no one else around. The crowing opera crowd had long since finished their spritzers and dispersed to their city centre penthouses and Nordend apartments. He followed his master down the steps to the passage beneath, where Ibra took off his pristine white shirt and handed it to Sajad. No words were exchanged. He understood that he should wear it. His own coat and shirt both stank and were filthy and torn. They would seduce no one. He pulled the clean shirt over his head, breathing the scent of good cologne deeply, then waited for instruction.

It was barely needed. It was to be the usual operation. Ibra waited below while Sajad went through the motions, above, automatically. His deadpan mimicry of sexual flirtation was now perfectly choreographed. A faultless homage to the black art of commerce, it contained everything it needed, all the codes and signifiers, and yet it meant nothing. The movement of body parts, the whisper of a word. All of it automatised in the service of a trick.

First, he found Marcel sitting, turning the ring, Gollum-like, on the edge of the grand but dormant fountain at the centre of the square. Next, he took a seat a few metres from him and opened his legs and rubbed his inner thigh. He looked at Marcel from under those long lashes and waited for eye contact. It took a moment or two for Marcel to notice him, a moment more for him to understand what was happening.

Marcel was confused and still a little drunk. The events of the night seemed unreal and bungled, but a part of him had expected it to end with sex. And now here was this boy. This boy who was looking at him. This boy who had come from nowhere, like in a dream. He had not made it with the whore, but now he felt arousal pawing. Maybe this was the thing to banish Simon? Someone else, whoever else, to make it go away, the thirst. His cock grew hard in his trousers as he watched the boy stand, unbutton his brilliant white shirt, then with a crooked finger, beckon Marcel to follow. Which he did. Willingly. Down, down. To Ibra, coiled.

They left him sobbing on the dirty floor and went to buy cheeseburgers. Ibra talked and talked, tossing the glinting ring up and down like a coin.

He shouted, "MacaDonalds, MacaDonalds," and laughed like an idiot child. He seemed really very happy. But Sajad could not rid himself of the picture of the man's sad eyes. The way they changed from shock, to desperation, to forlorn sadness. Sajad thought then of the dark Lake Urmia and those two sad moons, but still it had not been enough to move him to pity and shake him from his own stunned compliance. Nothing was, it seemed. He had simply stood there, holding the knife out level, letting his own dead eyes watch as Ibra took everything from the desperate stranger, then kicked him to a crumpled heap. He folded up the burgers into their brown bag and stuffed them into a coat pocket. He would eat them later, when the hunger came back.

Ibra explained, before they left the MacDonalds, what he wanted Sajad to do next. Sajad was told in a coarsely butchered mix of English and German, along with some crude gesturing, that he would bring the ring to Haus 69 at 16:00 hours the next day. He would bring it and present it to Ruby as Ibra's gift. He would wear the same shirt, Ibra's shirt. He would bow to her, when he handed it over. He nodded his agreement. He had understood. He did not ask why he should do these things and it did not matter to him to know. He was just very tired now and he wanted to get the man's sad eyes out of his head. He felt weak and he needed to sleep. A sleep, he hoped, without dreams.

Simon

There were few things that repulsed Simon Gravenreuth more than walking around the Bahnhofsviertal in Frankfurt in broad daylight. It was beneath him and he felt no hesitation in admitting that. The entire *umgebung* was an affront to his refined sense of aesthetics as well as a sick insult to his unrelenting fervour for commerce, which he liked to think of as being inextricably linked. Tramps, beggars, whores and junkies lounged on every filthy, piss-stained street corner like warts on the mouth of a grand old lady – simultaneously uglifying the gateway to the city he called his home and dragging down real estate prices by a truly ungodly ratio. He fucking hated the place. He hated the soft left, bleeding heart politicians in the *Staatsrat* even more for letting it exist.

Add to this the inconvenience of being bothered on a weekend, and you really were talking about some seriously thin fucking ice, but there was a principle at stake. One of his old friends – he and Marcel went way back – had been ripped off in the city by some skank, and he wasn't going to stand for it. He told Marcel to wait out front of his house. He'd pick him up in the new Porsche.

This Saturday afternoon, Kaiserstrasse, stretching from the Hauptbahnhof's splendid arches to the gauche, high rise grandeur of Willy Brandt Platz, looked especially revolting. It was an overcast day, sticky and warm, and the addled, unwashed zombies that permanently trawled the row of sex shops, dive bars, kiosks and kebab shops all wore the slovenly, sweat-stained malaise of a warm day on top of that thick robe of numbing intoxication that was their standard attire. They drifted around, indistinguishable from the litter they lived in. Simon would have held his fucking nose if he didn't despise such effeminate public gesturing even more than the shithole itself.

If he could have had his way, he'd have taken a water cannon to those streets and blasted off the scum. He'd close the guilt trip dreck-magnet that was the Bahnhof's Mission Addiction Programme and pack all the junkies off to some treatment centre in the suburbs. He'd buy out the pimps and the madams and sell their grand old houses to Chinese investment consortiums. Or Russians, whatever – people with real money. He'd close the kiosks and open conferencing centres, mid-range eateries, chain hotels. He'd have the place fucking sparkling.

"Another day for you and me in paradise," he said to the especially enfeebled, hung-over Marcel with a smug grin, as he swung the glistening chassis of his silver 911 into an exclusive, underground parking lot just parallel to the station, for which he paid an enormous premium. He was feeling particularly pleased with himself because of the apposite usage of a Phil Collins lyric. Retro and clever. Perfect.

Marcel was at his whining best. He'd been jumped by some thugs at a U-Bahn stop the night before and they'd taken his Grandma's ring, boo hoo, so he was feeling really very sorry for himself. Simon had heard the whole sorry story in a drip feed of lachrymose voicemail messages as he prepared a post-workout protein shake and he immediately felt sure the whore had something to do with it. He didn't trust whores. Or women generally, with the exception of his mother. He'd been ripped off by prostitutes in the past himself, so it was a brand of injustice he felt particularly keenly. It was just such an abuse of trust, so despite Marcel's pathetic protestations, Simon was determined to right some wrongs and show some people what's what.

It was nearly four in the afternoon. Most of the brothels and strip joints were not yet open, but they were making ready to be. Some seedier joints ran a programme of some sort of twenty-four hours a day, but Haus 69 was actually one of the more reputable brothels in the quarter, so the doors were still closed to guests. Simon himself had been there, many years ago, though before he'd made any serious cash.

As they approached the entrance, they saw a ragged group of pimpled youths disperse from the street corner, as though they'd rumbled some minor deal. Marcel began tugging on the hem of Simon's tight white T shirt and complaining again of how they should just go, leave it, how he didn't want a scene. It had the effect of further stretching the white cotton of Simon's top across the contours of his rippling chest and torso, framed perfectly in the afternoon light, but despite being secretly pleased by this, Simon shrugged off his mild-mannered friend and started to bang noisily on the door of the bordello. Marcel was a soft heart, but he had to know that a line had been crossed here. You couldn't have prostitutes and their ilk stealing family heirlooms from good, property owning folk without repercussions.

As Simon's large, pink fist hammered on the bolt locked plexiglass doors, he noticed one of the scrambled youths was still lurking at the corner, sizing him up. Or perhaps the little shit was ogling his conspicuously large, gold-plated Rolex. Smirking, he turned to face the boy, but as he did, the kid shot off down the street, before ducking into an alleyway some one-hundred yards along.

"That's odd," thought Simon. "I wonder if that *Kleine Assi* is running off to warn somebody – like some signalling system, or some shit…," but then he stopped thinking, because the door was opening and it was time for action.

Simon started straight in with trademark bluster. He talked down his nose at the bewildered doorman and insisted that they see the whore who called herself Ruby at once.

"We'll wait," he said, tapping the Rolex, wanting it to be noticed. "We've got all day." But when that tactic drew a flat rejection and an awkwardly silent, two-minute stand-off, he went straight to the angry rich boy playbook. He claimed to know people he didn't, he threatened to call the police, and he let it be known, so that the entire fucking Bahnhofsviertal was served notice, that unless they got that ring back by tonight, there would be some serious fucking consequences.

Yes, he caused precisely the sort of foot-stamping scene that Marcel had expected, and watching it, Marcel wondered if this wasn't secretly what he'd wanted to happen – despite his impotent protestations – just so he could bear witness to the irrational force majeure that was his big, blond friend bounding to his defence. He felt a surge of desire and even questioned if the words he heard Simon saying out loud, in the middle of one of Frankfurt's most notorious districts, could really be true. Did he, Marcel, really intend to propose to his girlfriend with his grandmother's ring at the Alte Oper that very night?

But Marcel was not the only witness to Simon's bravissimo performance. And he was not the only one wracked with doubt, either. Because just at that moment, Sophia stopped her passing taxi dead in the street, to step out with her baffled face wearing the question of why her partner's obnoxious best friend was so publicly bothering a brothel owner on a Saturday afternoon. Ruby watched nervously from her small boudoir window wondering exactly when Ibra would emerge with the treasure he'd promised. Ibra himself stepped from the alley with cold intent and a long blade concealed in a black sleeve, asking himself where on earth his boy was in all this confusion. And Sajad, who had been waiting patiently across the street in his bright white shirt the whole time, clutching the ring in his sweating right palm, heard the sound of a police siren, then turned and ran.

Ha ha. Yes! You enjoy? I mean, is sad, yes, but good? Like opera. Black opera... like ink over the many golden rings of a fat pig banker's hands. You find hard to believe? Ha ha. By God in these forgotten parts, always on show, is normal, I tell you. And Sajad – poor Sajad – is good boy, no? You like him too? You should. He brought me shoes one time – I swear on every god I know and the many I don't. Good shoes. Leather. Good as my coat, by God and Dr Martin! And he ask no money! No joke. He is really very good boy.

But this no fairy story. This much darker. Things may not end well for him, or any of us, you understand? It is normal. Bad things are normal. Good people, bad things. So what? Love, rings, hope... they get swapped and sold here, every day. People too. In big towers made from cash. In gutter full with tears. This place – if you listen – it is full of these songs – sussshh – listen to that old lady cry. How sad, yes? NO! Sorry, not to stop. Not now. Lubo mean no harm. You good lady, good man. You go on your way. On with your story. I come back later. You listen good. Maybe you find some truthings, yes? OK? Shush.

***

Sophia

Sophia left the meeting at the Intercontinental hotel and stepped hurriedly into a taxi from the waiting rank outside. She gave the home address that she ordinarily shared, despite his non-appearance that past evening, with her partner Marcel and gnawed distractedly on the well-chewed top of a biro she had been using to take notes all that stuffy but potentially life changing afternoon.

Her thick hazel eyebrows furrowed as she looked out on the snaking traffic that swept around the corner past the Hauptbahnhof and then onto Mainzer Landstrasse, heading out of town. Hoping to make it home as quickly as possible, only in order that she should make herself beautiful for a performance of *Wagner* she in no way wanted to attend, she told the driver to take a quick right and left, crossing Kaiserstrasse as they went, to circumvent the snarl up ahead. She tapped her foot anxiously, rapped her spindly fingers against the leather seat and chewed on the pen top a little more.

What was bothering Sophia into a full display of her numerous and irritating nervous ticks was not Marcel's recent erratic behaviour, or that she didn't much like opera, or even that her man had apparently spent all night in the company of a friend, Simon, who she genuinely hated. What was bothering Sophia was the meeting she had just come from.

In it, Sophia had been offered a job she desperately wanted but that, if taken, meant turning upside down the life she and Marcel – and his mother, Merle, for that matter – had built together. Her current role was secure and very well remunerated. It gave her freedom to work from anywhere she chose and salary that could support the ailing Kleemeyer family business. But it was utterly soulless. In reality, it was no more than an exercise in greenwashing. Privately, she called her team, the sustainability branch of a leading cosmetics firm, the *goat head* of the company. A friendly, vegan, animal loving face, that helped the firm turn out – then widely publicise – a product or two per year with a minimal carbon footprint, using newly researched, environmentally neutral ingredients. Meanwhile, the snakes in marketing fed the profit-turning lions of product development, who were, in reality, the brains and belly of the beast. They went on mass-producing billions of cubic tonnes of old favourites every day: lotions, creams, pastes and gels, you name it. And they gulped down palm oil and belched out pollutants like the thirsty chimera they really were. It literally stank.

Fatigued by that creeping, familiar soul rot that seemed to her to be part of the package with adulthood, Sophia had long wanted to quit; do something she believed in. If it hadn't been for the debt she felt she owed to Marcel's mother she would have done so long ago. Now, finally, was the offer of a job that could really make a difference: A research partnership led by Humboldt University. A sustainable product development, with the goal of establishing a model for future manufacture in developing economies. Something real. Something decent. It was exactly what she had studied for. But the role was in Berlin, and for half the money that she currently earned.

It would mean no more propping up the property company that Merle had tried so long, however blunderingly, to keep afloat. It would mean leaving the city that Marcel so loved and starting again, with no guarantee that he would follow her. But what was more troubling than the prospect of all these terrible upheavals, was the fact that deep down, she was desperate for just this kind of a way out.

Sophia knew only too well that Marcel was planning to propose to her, and she knew too that she would have to say no. The only thing she was unsure of was how she should tell her fragile, funny soulmate of all these years her answer? How many reasons were enough? How much detail was too much? People say that honesty is always the best policy, but that only proves what idiots people are. Honesty, in truth, is almost always a brutal, bruising business.

How do you tell a man you still, in some ways at least, love that it isn't – and never will be – enough? How do you tell him that the plans you have been making – secretly, fervently, passionately – no longer have him as part of them? Or that the affection of his mother, though you care for her very much, is a weight you can no longer bear? How do you tell a man you have been sleeping with for more than a decade that finally, absurdly, almost certainly, you think he may be gay?

Out of this crowding of questions, a strange sort of answer loomed suddenly and bewilderingly into view. As her cab intersected the red-light district and passed the corner of Kaiserstrasse with its infamous Haus 69, she saw Simon in the doorway, his square head a-bobbing with its idiotic shock of blond as he gesticulated wildly in the direction of her cowed and sheepish would-be fiancé.

"Stop!" shouted Sophia, just in time to see a police car swerve into the junction and a young man in a bright white shirt sprint suddenly from the scene.

Sajad

When he stopped running, he was at the river. He hadn't meant to go there. It was just where the panic had brought him. Gasping for air, he threw himself down on a bench that overlooked the Main river and started to sob.

He could not say why he was crying. There were no reasons for his actions anymore. He realised he had become a thing without a soul, moved only by threat and the instinctive mechanisms that followed. Why should he run from the police? What thing could they do to him that was worse than how he already lived?

On the river, a long cargo boat sailed quietly by, and he watched it part the dark water effortlessly. He should have drowned in that lake. God had kept him alive just to mock him. People passed by and regarded him strangely, but no one asked him what the matter was. No one offered to help. Perhaps they were afraid. Afraid of his black hair and dark features, his dirty face streaked with tears, his piercing eyes, wet and raw. Perhaps they were just afraid, as people so often are, of someone feeling something so strongly that they cannot understand.

Letting the sobs subside, he dried his tears with a bitter snort on his master's white sleeve and took the ring from his pocket. His first instinct was to throw it into the river and let it sink. He could do it just to spite the devil he'd come to serve and despise. "Let him dive for it," he thought, "if it means so much to him.

Let it be added to my never-ending bill." But something stopped him. He held it up to the light to look at it properly for the first time. It was a thing of great beauty and, he realised, it must have been of great value too.

He brought it close to his face to study it more closely. What could he get for this thing? How might it change his own fate? Could money alone save a person's soul, or did all rich people become like his master? As he looked at the ring more closely, he was moved not by the beauty of the red stones, or the lustre of the golden hue, but by a tiny inscription that ran around the inside of the band. He did not understand the lettering – it was from an alphabet he had never seen before. But he understood that this ring truly meant something. It stood for something, maybe even for some*one*.

What did he stand for now? Who or what did he represent? Piecing together the tiny lines and dashes of the unfamiliar engraving, the realisation dawned on him that he had not really thought for himself since he was a child. In school, or with his family, he had only ever done what was expected of him. He had carried the expectation of others, first that he would provide for them in whichever way was required, then that he would go to Europe and find them riches. In Europe, he would be safe, so went the story – so safe and so rich that he could bring them all to him, out of Kandahar, out of want, out of danger, for the rest of their days. But these were not his thoughts. They were only the ones he had received, never thinking to question them.

"So," he asked again, "what now?" He tried to make himself quiet. He tried, for the first time in his life, perhaps, to still the fear, the anger, the desperate traffic of instinct and panic that often passed for thought – and listened for an answer that came from some place true. And what he heard was faint and indistinct, like the inscription itself, spoken in a whisper.

"Give it back," it sighed, and he knew what that meant. Give. It. Back. He knew then what he must try, at least, to do.

It was no easy thing, of course, though the message was clear. It meant he would have to return to that place, to Alte Oper, his own Hell, that very night, where his master would be waiting. He would have to go there alone and, if he could, try to find the man with sad eyes, to give back what they'd taken. He'd have to do all that before his master could find him and take both himself and the ring back into his possession. But something told him it was important to try, despite the risk. It was, perhaps, the most important thing he would ever do. He had to follow his own instinct, now that he had finally let it speak. He had to do something right.

For the next few hours, Sajad walked by the river and thought about home. He thought of the prayer calls rising on warm nights like this over the domed mausoleum of the old town, the scent of roasted lamb drifting in the aisles of the Pashtun bazaars. He took a crusty cheeseburger from his pocket and, as he ate, he wondered what his brothers and sisters were doing at that moment. Were they making the same journey he had made? Was anyone coming to look for him? He hoped not.

He sat on a high wall by a railway bridge and smoked the bits of cigarette he found on the floor. He let the hours pass by like the rumbling of trains behind him.

"There is no sound sadder than a train in the night," he thought. "But there is no sound more hopeful, either." He liked such thoughts – the ones that don't make sense but are true anyway. He smiled to himself. As the lazy traffic of the idling city passed behind him and the river made its way slowly to the distant sea beneath his dangling legs, he watched, through the clearing clouds, the orange sun set over the Taunus hills. Night was approaching. Another night in this hard, foreign place. For once, though, he did not feel hungry and he did not feel tired. He did not feel scared, either, though he probably should have done. When it was time, he simply stood and walked back through the town at an even pace, as though being drawn by a current to a distant shore. He felt a stillness settle within him like the arrival of the cloudless night itself. He stepped onto the square at Opern Platz just in time.

It was 11 o'clock and the doors were opening to let out the esteemed guests. Somewhere amongst them was the man with the sad eyes. He walked to the middle of the crowd and waited. He let God decide what would happen next. Would he first see Ibra, his master, who would surely be hanging, shark-like, suspended in the rushing tide of oncoming suits? Or would he see the man with his unmistakable sadness? The wave came towards him. It broke and swirled. He swayed and watched, a white moon high above. And then, from the sea of faces, was one he recognised.

Ibra saw Sajad and smiled. Sajad did not smile back, but obediently, he walked toward his master. Their eyes were fixed on each other as they drew ever closer, until Sajad, breaking, lowered his gaze to the ground, deflated. Ibra smiled again as he cut through the crowd and he nodded to Sajad as he went. He was smiling at his servant because he was happy with him. He was happy because he was sure of what he was bringing him. Things were always brought to him, in the end. They were placed at his feet. This ring was no different.

But Ibra was wrong. Sajad no longer had the ring. He was bringing something else to his master. Just moments before seeing Ibra, Sajad had caught the slightest glimpse of the man from the U-bahn klo, the man from the street, the man with those terribly sad eyes – holding the hand of his lover, who also seemed overcome with emotion, for there were tears in her eyes too. And silently, as they passed, like fishes in a current, Sajad had slipped the ring into the pocket of its owner, quite undetected, whispered an apology, then let them drift on by.

Now he walked towards Ibra to return something else. He walked towards his master to give him what he deserved. And as they closed on each other, Sajad's eyes still aimed at the ground, he waited for his master's rough hands to take him by his collar and pull him close, like the first time they met. And when he felt that grip, the hot breath on his face and his body being drawn in, dragged and forced, claimed like a possession, he returned not the ring, but the knife he had been given that very first night. With force, with thanks, he returned the blade into his captor's gut.

"God is good," he whispered into Ibra's ear, as the tall man crumpled and fell, stunned by shock and crippled with pain, his dark eyes blinking with disbelief. And when Sajad pulled back the blade and felt the rush of something warm across his trembling hand, he knew he had done something good, something right. And not for the first time, and not for the last, Sajad ran.

***

Ha hhaaaaaa! Yes! I know. Is crazy, yes? Little Sajad – what a guy, by every god and minister together in a bastard pot! Where he go? Where little Sajad run to? I cannot to tell. Perhaps he running still? Maybe resting somewhere, like rich man, on tax-free islands? I hope. I hope.

But wait, you are saying, seeing me suddenly, down here, interested now, because of this thing that I have, what has grab your attentions. How you, Lubo? How now you have the ring? It was dropped in good boy Marcel's pocket, no? Full circle, yes? Right back where it start, where it belong, yes? No? Yes?

But I told you, deep down, Marcel is good boy man. And when good boy man sees poor beggar man on edge of rich person's crowd – yoo hooo, down here – with excellent coat but no monies in his cups – then good boy man is must to give. Is shame. Is shame. But true. And you rich men and women carry so much change in those good, hand stitching pockets. So, you maybe perhaps not always pay attention to what you drop in hands of man like Lubo. And tonight, this excellent night – with a high moon and hot wind

– tonight Marcel is reach in pocket, and drop everything what is there, ring included, plop, inside my strong tower of plastic cups, which is really very, very generous, must to say.

So here I am. In midnight alley. With special ring. You like how it sings? I on way to Bahnhofsviertal, which is really very dirty place, though I have these strong shoes. Is place with whores and pawn shops and trains to far off places and bad men with blade and good girls with dream. But you is no need for asking what is happen next. No no. God in heaven with a famous hat. You know for sure where I am heading, right? Nice lady, nice man. You know me by now? Of course you do. Is Lubo. Nice to meet.

Good Night Drinks

It was the start of another uncertain summer vacation. It was to be my last one in Cologne, though I hadn't let anyone know that yet. I hadn't even admitted it to myself, though I think by then I had a pretty good idea. The job was four years old and I hadn't liked it in the first place: teaching English in a posh private school for the kids of business types and Anglo-orientated expats, I told myself it had never been a good fit for my anarcho-communist worldview, whilst thanking my lucky stars for the more than competitive salary that had saved me from a spiralling debt problem. To my own surprise I was forty, sober, out of the woods, bored and – in the bittersweet meanwhile – another Big Love had bloomed then withered on the vine. Sarah. Another story – and one that, since I'm not entirely ready to tell it, we'll leave for another time.

Suffice to say we had remained friends and, uncomfortably, flatmates. She was German and direct and had explained how it simply didn't make economic sense for us to give up the place in Rodenkirchen and settle for separate places that would undoubtedly be much smaller. Germans seem to place a lot of importance on quadrat meters and I had to admit, for what we had, it was a steal. Plus, in the back of my mind was this sense that

I wouldn't be there long. I just quietly went along with it, but what it did mean was I was spending more time out of the flat, seeking out running clubs and conversation groups and such that didn't call for meeting in bars, drinking in bars, falling out of bars – or didn't call for *only* that, anyway. I'd been more or less dry for six months at the time and was determined to stay that way. I suppose what I'm saying is that I was in a strange place altogether. Not vulnerable exactly, but suggestible. Suggestible and restless. That might go some way towards explaining the way things panned out.

Robert contacted me on Messenger on a Wednesday night. He wrote, and here I can quote him directly as I still have the message chain sitting there in my inbox. Curiously, I think of it as evidence, though evidence for what I don't quite know. Anyway, he wrote:

"Hey hombre. I'm having some leaving drinks on Sunday. Want to come over and wish me goodbye?"

Now, this message seemed strange for two reasons. Firstly, I didn't really know Robert. We had met twice in total. He was the captain of a quaint little running club, Kraft Runners, which I now see was an intentional *wortwitz* – a play on words. *Kraft* means 'force' in German, but to the largely ex-pat community in Robert's little club it clearly stood for something else. I stopped attending after it became obvious that it was just a front for Robert's real passion: Koelsch beer.

The runs would start and end at a kiosk on Severinstrasse that boasted an impressive array of refrigerated beverages, and both times I attended Robert was drinking before the run, which was, even by Koelnisch standards, fairly unusual. He was a funny guy. He had a youthful face and wispy strawberry blond hair that made me think of a grown-up boy scout, with a pot belly accentuated by the skin-tight Lycra of his outfit and the bumbag he wore to carry the subs.

The runs were short and breathy and low on numbers. His tight T-shirt had the word *Captain* in large letters on the back. I met Roland there both times: an amicable, balding fifty-something German who shared Robert's Koelsch enthusiasm, though he limited his drinking to post-run *stange* sinking. I also remember a boastful Texan with a dyed black ponytail and an angry looking goatee beard who called himself Pyro. The guy was in bad shape and couldn't run for shit, but you wouldn't have known that to hear him talk. He was one of those *all the gear and no idea* types. There must have been others, though I can't remember them. What I do remember is there were never more than five on a run and, as I was trying to kick the drink, the atmosphere after exercise was boozily counterproductive. I swapped numbers with Robert and, thinking little of it, I joined his Facebook group too. I assumed that would be the end of it.

The second strange thing about the message was its phrasing. 'I'm having'. 'Wish me…' This focus on the singular. Something about Robert's nervous energy on our two previous meetings, the way he joked endlessly and added his own reflexive laugh after each punchline, led me immediately to suspect that it was entirely possible, were I to attend, that I might be the only guest at these goodbye drinks. Which were to happen *where* exactly? At his home? 'Come over' implies a home invite, I guessed. It seemed odd to invite a stranger to your home having only met them twice. Which, of course, should have been enough. Having pegged the guy for a crank and then to receive this odd invite, some months after our last meeting, well, that should have been all the information I needed to make my excuses and flat bat the guy. But I didn't. I put it by Sarah. She didn't waste any words.

"What? That weird guy from the running dingsbums? No. I would not go there. He could murder you. Just tell him you're busy. You can blame it on me if you want. Say you have plans with your 'girlfriend' or something. I don't care."

"Yeah." I said, biting on my bottom lip. Sarah often said, "I don't care," when she meant "I don't mind." It was just a little thing, but it bothered me.

So, I wrote Robert back. "Yeah, I could be free. Send me the address. Word of warning though, I'm still off the booze. I'll bring my own refreshment."

"Cool. No worries. We can accommodate! Steinstrasse 29, 'bout 9ish." The breeziness in his reply was offset by how immediately it was bounced back to me. It did put me at ease a little though. I didn't think about it too much for the next couple of days. Then, on Sunday, I got another message.

"We on for tonight then?" and a picture of some beer chilling in a fridge. I thought, "Fuck it, it could be interesting." That's really what I thought. That kind of selfish thought that sometime writers have where everything could be the inspiration for a story, though they usually end up as little more than a rarely told anecdote. I left the flat around eight. I didn't mention to Sarah where I was going.

I cycled over and chained the bike up some distance from his place. I stopped in at a kiosk and bought a bottle of wine on autopilot. I was early. I went and sat in a bar for fifteen minutes and sipped on a Coke. The bar was weirdly quiet. Then I slowly strolled down the road and buzzed on his buzzer. There was a stillness in his street too. A blanket of stillness that hummed just a little with the tension of the city and the heat of the day radiated through asphalt and concrete. It was the kind of summer stillness that should mean contentment, or potential or something. Robert buzzed me in.

"Top floor, hombre…" he said. I pushed the door open and made my way up.

Unsurprisingly, Robert was alone when I arrived, a little out of breath.

I thought, "Well, there you go. What did you expect?" Panting, I held out the bottle of wine I'd brought as a present and scanned the hallway for anything weird. Everything was normal. There were pictures of Robert and a woman I assumed was his wife, and pictures of children too, on a sideboard, though I couldn't study them closely. It was getting late and it was already quite gloomy. There were a few large pairs of shoes on a shoe rack.

"HOMBRE!" he said, taking the wine, ushering me along the hallway, "Naughty! You shouldn't have…"

He showed me through a large kitchen-lounge, stylishly furnished, and out onto a wide, square balcony that was actually more like a terrace.

"Quadrat meters," I thought, enjoying the view from the fifth floor. It looked out onto the coiled back streets of Cologne, almost all of them rebuilt from ashes in the middle of last century, in the direction of the Heumarkt, and of course, those famous twin spires of the city's beloved *Dom*. Mercifully, it had been the only thing left standing after our countrymen had flattened the place some seventy years ago in the name of freedom. I had always liked to think there was something noble and tender in such an obvious act of mercy, until a colleague from school, a history teacher, suggested it was spared only because of its utility as a point of navigation for the American and English bombers. Less poetical than strategic, then, although I cling to the hope that the reality was somewhere in between. At the edge of the balcony there was a small table with just two chairs on either side. Cold beers beaded with condensation sat temptingly in the middle of the table. Robert had chilled some alcohol-free ones, too, which I thought was a nice touch.

I sat and continued scanning my surroundings as Robert cracked open a bottle for me and placed it in my right hand. The warm air from the embers of midsummer and my exertions in climbing his *altbau* staircase had combined to leave me feeling woozy. It wasn't an unpleasant feeling and I found that, far from the awkwardness I'd anticipated, I felt quite at home sitting there on Robert's balcony. I decided to make the best of it and go on as though we really were friends.

"So, what's with the move? Where you headed?" I asked, sipping on my cool weizen and only slightly wishing it was the real thing.

He flopped down a passport with a ticket tucked conspicuously inside the cover. The ticket had a code I didn't understand, and it was inside a British passport. I was surprised he still had one. From the little I'd learned of him I'd gathered he'd lived in Germany for close to twenty years.

"Vilnius!" He said, "Where the wife hails from. She wants the boys to be closer to her family, which I understand, and our work you can do anywhere, right, so… yeah: Vicious Vilnius! The old nag of Europe… the city I mean, not the wife! Ha ha."

That laugh again. It made me smile. Then something puzzled me.

"I'm sorry, 'our work'?" I asked, "What is it you do again?" I could vaguely remember explaining between exerted puffs the various reasons I disliked my job on the last run we'd taken. It had become a habit when meeting strangers that past year, a regrettable and somewhat reckless one, but I hadn't gathered that he taught too.

"Yeah, I teach English, man. Like you. Business English and Translation – at least that's what the card says. Ha ha!"

"Oh, right! Well, here's to you…" I raised my bottle in his direction and he cracked open his own beer and took a long pull. He smiled at me in a way that lingered a little, then he wiped his mouth suddenly and looked away. I envied him, to have a new destination already settled, the surety of family in waiting and I thought of my own strange situation with a percolating sense of dread. I was supposed to be past this kind of thing by now, this uncertainty, this floating around in and out of people's lives. Men of my age were supposed to have direction, structure, a foundation into which the congealing mass of old age could be poured and fill up all the gaps. Learning suddenly that Robert, a man I'd considered, at least on some level, to be a little silly, had an apparently better handle on these fundaments than I did was unsettling. I was surprised to find that he was also an English teacher. That was something I would usually make a mental note of. I'd had him down for something techie in the banking sector and felt sure that he'd told me that himself, but what the hell, I thought. Bloody English teachers. There's enough of us around.

We sat there just drinking our beers together like a couple of fellas for a minute or two. As we did, the sun finally ducked below the line of houses and the inkiness of night started to creep down from the heavens and up from the alleyways, snaring the day in its well-rigged trap. Robert suddenly sprang to his feet.

"Oh, nachos! Nachos for the hombres!" And he disappeared inside then returned shortly after carrying a bowl of tortilla chips slathered with a noxious looking yellow-orange sauce. He seemed to be doing things on autopilot, as though they were part of some plan. I wondered how many beers he'd drunk before my arrival. But he smiled that big insistent smile at me and motioned for me to take one of the nachos, so I did, out of politeness. The luminous dip tasted better than it looked.

"So," I began, working compounded tortilla chip out of a molar with my tongue and eager to get at least one of the questions that had been bothering me off my chest, "no work mates, tonight? No one from Kraft Runners?"

"Oh, you didn't hear about Kraft?" he asked, ignoring the first part of my question. "I thought I added you to the group?"

It was true that I had involuntarily been made a part of some WhatsApp group or other where the members of the running club communicated, but I had muted it almost immediately and rarely bothered to check the to and fro. I had no idea what he was talking about.

"They asked me to leave," said Robert. "Asked me to leave my own club! Can you believe that?!"

I said nothing and waited for him to go on.

"They said they didn't like the new rules. Pyro, that prick, he was the ringleader. I made a new rule saying everyone had to drink. After a run, everyone had to stay for at least one drink, yeah? Alcoholic or otherwise…" Here he nodded at me, his bug eyes popping, "For the social element, yeah? Just half an hour, you know? And maybe I got a bit angry when they tried to leave early, because that's not fair… right… if you're in a club? And they didn't like it. Said I was dictating the fun. And that the runs weren't long enough. And blah, blah, blah. Pricks. So, I told them to go fuck themselves. Ha ha. Told them I'd start a new club, in Vilnius or wherever. Those pricks. Just like back in Millfield."

Letting the final, cryptic reference with its unmistakable flavour of deep lying bitterness slide, I picked up another tortilla chip and ate it, then grabbed another two or three to keep in hand as they really were much better than they'd looked. I tried my best to keep the atmosphere casual.

"Seems a shame," I said and shrugged.

"Ppfft. Shame, shame, know your name, right? Ha ha. Nah, fuck those guys. Who needs 'em?

They're not like us, right? We're cool, right, hombre?"

He was bugging at me again. Considering that their mutiny was organised along the exact same objections I'd had to Robert's venture, I decided to keep schtum and move the conversation on to neutral ground.

"These tortilla chips are really very good," I said.

"Oh yeah, you like those? There's more inside. As much as you want. What about comics, huh? Hombre? You like comics too? I bet you do."

I don't really like comics, not in the way 'people who like comics' like comics, but something about the note of pleading in Robert's voice told me I had to give him something.

"Sure," I said. "I love comics."

"Cos that's going to be my new thing. In Vilnius or wherever. Comics. A comic club. Comics and running. I'll combine them both. What do you think?"

"That, erm, could work," I said, though the precise opposite thought was ruminating. How could that work? You read comics then go running all geed up on heroism? Where do you put the

171

comics in all that Lycra? Or you run first then read comics, all sweaty, to chill out? It sounded silly but clearly, he was enthusiastic enough about the idea for the both of us. His eyes had taken on a distant quality and he was smiling to himself.

"Yeah," he said to himself, reverently, "it's like I tell my girls. You're never alone with a good comic. You've got all kinds of friends, heroes even, right there. Your very own gang."

Suddenly, that anticipated sense of unease climbed jangling down from the eaves and squatted evilly over the moment. A silent alarm within me stiffened my back as the darkness of the evening drew itself tight around our little table. Why *were* the back streets of a city in summer so quiet that night? Where was the dispassionate, inconsequential clatter of close quarter lives to disturb and reassure? My own breath felt cooler in my lungs. Robert himself seemed unaware of the sudden atmospheric chill, still gazing into the middle distance, hauntologically warmed by his vision of an as-yet-unfounded Lithuanian sports and literature club.

"Girls?" I asked, attempting to remain breezy, but measuring my words, "I thought you said you had boys?"

"What?" asked Robert, startled. "Oh, yes! Boys! My boys. Sorry. The girls are… you know… I teach some girls. The English classes. Sometimes I get confused myself!"

The answer made little sense. He'd said 'my girls'. That seemed too familiar for students. And Business English students? They are almost invariably adults. What child needs to learn Business English? Robert grinned at me. I started trying to connect some of the other information I'd gathered that night. The photos. The shoe rack. I pushed myself back in my chair and opened the angle so that I sat side on, facing the open glass slide door to the lounge and the hall beyond, and the staircase beyond that. Robert was a small man and I judged myself a stone or two heavier than he was. Ten kilos, maybe, in the metric measurements I'd never quite adapted to. I knew from our previous outings I had more than his measure of stamina too. Calibrations and calculations of this kind started happening together, all at once, without so much as the flickering of an eyelid. I thought of Sarah, alone, in our awkwardly shared flat and felt a little pang of regret. It occurred to me then that I hadn't asked Robert the most obvious question of all.

"And where are they? Your wife and kids, I mean? Where are they tonight?"

I was thinking of that shoe rack. There had been no children's shoes.

"Oh, those guys. They're out. Erika, my wife, she took them to see friends. They may even sleep over. They often do."

Robert delivered this report flatly, which on one level made it sound quite plausible but, at the same time, like something rehearsed. It was more the way he looked at me, though. He stared back at me with a gaze that seemed to dare contradiction, and I'd seen it before. In my line of work, you see it often, on the faces of unrepentant teenagers bearing down a transgression they have no intention of confessing. It felt unpleasant to be experiencing it now, dislocated, from a man I took to be my own age and in his own home too. I wondered what constellation of deceits lay behind it in Robert's case. But, just as suddenly as it had arrived, his expression changed again, animated now into a great big bug-eyed smile at whatever idea seemed to be occurring to him at that very moment.

"Ooooh, cocoa!" He said, delightedly. "Is it getting cold? Do you feel cold? I can make us some cocoa and you can check out my comics."

I decided this should be my cue to leave. As curious as I was about the nature of what was happening, I was unnerved by Robert's jumpiness and had Sarah's warning ringing in my ears.

"Robert," I said, "it's getting late. I really should…"

"No, no, nono, no noooo," he said. "No bother, hombre! I've got some made up. Follow me."

And before I could say anything he had sprung out of his chair and disappeared inside again. I waited. And I waited. The strange stillness that had hung in the air all night now seemed instead to radiate from the dark patch of black doorway that Robert had ducked into. I waited a little longer. I kept my eyes fixed there on the doorway for a while. I kept expecting him to spring suddenly back out with more snacks, a Lego set, a skipping rope or a fucking samurai sword. But he did not reappear and so, as calmly as I could, I stood and began to walk, slowly but purposefully, towards the lounge door, intending – hoping – to walk straight through it, along that hallway and leave for good.

It was ten o' clock. With just about my first step, the ominous tolling of the cathedral bells started up. It was perfect. I was seized by a sudden desire to laugh out loud but silenced myself and, playing my role of victim in a silent movie as well as I could, began to synchronise my near theatrical steps with each sound of the distant bells. I stepped inside the flat and the bells kept tolling. When they stopped, I stopped too and looked about. I was in the middle of Robert's lounge but he was nowhere to be seen. It was very dark inside. I could no longer make out any of the pictures on the walls and sideboards, but a glow came from the hallway and I could see halfway down that one door was open to a room lit with an orange light.

The strange thing is that it did not make me feel scared. There was fear, yes, the measured, intrepid fear of the unknown. He was in there. Doing… something. Waiting for me, in some way, whatever that meant. But there was no panic. In fact, I was drawn to it, the open door. And that is why, instead of striding deliberately past and slamming the front door shut behind me as I'd planned, I started to draw myself up slowly, encroaching with small steps, getting closer to the glowing, open doorway.

"Robert," I called out in my most masculine, teacherly voice as I approached the last few steps, "I think, like I said, I'm going to head off now. I don't want to disturb you anymore."

"No, wait…" came the voice, tiny, meek and needy.

I placed my left hand on the frame of the door to steady myself and leaned my head inside. I had to dam a surge of laughter from bursting from my lips. Robert was in bed. Across the other side of the room, in the farthest right corner as I looked, Robert was wearing blue cotton pyjamas and a sleeping hat and had an Avengers bed spread pulled up to his waist. In his hands he was cupping a mug of something and to his side, his left, beneath the warm glow of a bedside lamp, was a red stool – a stack of classic looking comics was perched on top.

The sweet smell of warm milk drifted over to the doorway and I could see, at the foot of the stool, Robert had prepared a drink for me too. It steamed, temptingly. The floor between us was strewn with comics and action figures. On the wood effect walls were posters of classic heroes, some fictional, some real, tacked up by coloured pins with all the care and attention of a fan who is old enough to know better. It did not look so much like the bedroom of a young boy, so much as a museum to a young boy's past.

"Read some comics to me," he said, his voice small and wavering, but with no hint of malice, and just the slightest note of resignation. I looked into his eyes and I could see everything as it was. There were no wife and children. This room, unmistakably, was his room. He was a lonely man who just wanted some company. Robert began hurriedly to explain how lonely he'd been at boarding school, where he'd been bullied, and how all he'd ever wanted then was an older brother to look after him and maybe sometimes read some comics with. His voice was nervous and rushed, as if he could sense some tiny flame of opportunity flickering out, and that his words might keep it alive if he just kept talking. I waved a hand for him to stop. For the second time that night, I thought,

"Fuck it. What harm can it do? Before anyone knows, we'll both be gone from here."

"Robert," I said, "I'll read one comic and then I'm going home." I was still being teacher, but the kindly type now. "I hope you can accept that."

"Oh, hombre, yes… I mean, that's great," he said. "Thank you. *Thank* you."

I walked over to his side of the room and stooped down. Gingerly, I moved the comics to one side, and I sat in the stool he'd positioned by the side of his bed. Then I picked up one of the comics. It was *Batman and Robin*. I looked down at the large, homely mug of brown liquid.

"Drink it. Go on. It's just cocoa, hombre. Just a nice cup of cocoa like matron never thought to fucking make. Ha ha."

I had to laugh now too. I laughed a short but hard laugh, shaking my head – ha! – then I took the cup and lifted it to my mouth. I took a sip. I can't say how much was just the moment, the surprise of having macabre expectations met, then confounded, then met again – but it seemed to me then – and still does in my recollection – that it was the most delicious cup of cocoa I have ever tasted. It tasted like contentment, or potential or something. I began to read.

I read the action bits with gusto and tilted the comic in Robert's direction so he could see the pictures. I did voices for the characters. I really got into them. I did a deep, Midwest, growly type voice for Batman; a chirpy New Yorker style for Robin. From his reaction, it seemed like I was getting it just right. The soft orange light was reflected in his face and twinkled magically in his bug eyes until, finally, as I approached the end of the caper, they drew sleepily closed. I put the comic down on the floor, shaking my head a little at what had just happened, and went to leave.

I stopped suddenly as I rose and turned, because standing there in the bedroom doorway, holding the hands of two young boys, was an attractive looking woman wearing a beige summer jacket. She must have been in her thirties. She had a weary, drawn look on her face that spoke of disappointment without surprise. I had the feeling she wasn't looking at me at all. She was staring straight through me. She looked, truth be told, utterly worn out.

"Robert," she said, firmly, "this has got to stop."

Epilogue
One Day in September

Before I start anything, I should say, this isn't a short story. It isn't one on two accounts. First of all, most short stories are made up and this is real, it happened, as should be obvious to anyone. Secondly, it doesn't go anywhere, really. Not in the way you might expect a short story to really go somewhere – with a plot and such. But it is real, a sort of a memoir, and it is about me and my Nan, a remarkable woman who I loved and is long dead, so it means something, I hope, and maybe not just to me, which is the reason I am writing it down.

It was early September 2001, and I was staying at my Nan's house in Childwall, Liverpool before the start of the university term. It was a regular thing I did then – staying there before the term started up. I'd spend the best part of each summer in Germany. My folks still lived there, in Osnabrück, so I´d doss with them: saving money, behaving better and enjoying the pilsner, the sun and the open-air swimming baths. Good clean fun. But I was always eager just to get back to Liverpool and spend a week with my Nan and, if I am completely honest, start drinking heavily again before any of my uni mates were back and at it too. Getting the jump on them, I liked to think. That's exactly how I thought of it in my smug, clever-idiot head – like some trick or stunt I was pulling. I'd drink with my cousins, sometimes alone, down in the late summer-emptied university bars, and brag about it later when my housemates turned up. I'd call them lightweights, that kind of thing, which was really fucking absurd and said a great deal about me and where I was then, and for some time after, but there you go.

It was brilliant. I was twenty years old and I didn't have a care. I'd spent the previous six months recovering from a broken heart that had caused me to drink even more heavily for a short while and then drop out of my second year of uni. I deferred the year, in fact, rather than drop out altogether. I was never brave enough for that kind of total abandon, thank god. The rest of that half-abandoned year I'd been working pretty much full-time as a *shoe troll* in a department store in town, so I'd saved some money and I was all set to repeat the year and really fucking ace it this time – and I did as it turns out, though by my own relatively modest standards. I got some kind of bursary, forty quid I think, for being in the top ten students that year, which I lost pretty much immediately thanks to short-term loan library fines. I'm telling you all this only because it helps to set the scene, but also because who doesn't like a humble-brag from time to time? Rest assured, I shat out of a number of modules in my third year, ending up with a pretty average 2:1. I am not, never was, one of those deeply unsympathetic high-flier types – so it's absolutely okay to enjoy the rest of the story, or whatever it is we didn't fully decide this actually is.

Nan would have been in her mid-seventies at the time. Her name was Mary, but I didn't often hear her called that and never used her name myself. It was usually Nan, Mam, Girl, Queen even – but on the odd occasion somebody would use her real name, usually an aunty of mine, saying "Sit down, Mary, let me do that…" or something, I'd be struck always by how it sounded.

Strange. Rare. Proper. Though none of these things were really true. Mary is a common enough name, after all.

On this afternoon, the afternoon of the 11th of September, I was lying in bed nursing a bruising hangover, which was not unusual, as I think I've made clear. I'd been out with one of my cousins, Ess, the night before. I'd got so drunk that I couldn't remember much of what had happened but felt sure that I'd done something awful and had already accepted that we would probably avoid each other for the next year or so until memory relented, and we decided to repeat the trick again. I reached my hand down between my legs to check the sheets and breathed a heavy sigh of relief. No tell-tale dampness. I rolled over onto my side and painfully, gingerly, I opened one eye and groaned. There was a compressed polystyrene box on the floor next to my bed, splattered with an evil-looking scarlet sauce, bits of drying lettuce and stinking of donner meat. A thin blade of pale light striped my face where it came through a crack in the door from the landing.

I was sleeping in the small spare room right at the top of the stairs, which had no radiator. In fact, I'm not even sure the house had central heating at all. This room, however, was particularly famous in our family for its cold. You could see your breath and that was in the summer, my father often joked. As a result, my nose was cold, but my mouth was sandpaper dry from all the drink. I was dying for a piss too. I knew I had to get out of bed, though I would have gladly taken death as a preferred option if there'd been a way to do it without experiencing discomfort or inconveniencing anyone. I could hear my Nan pottering downstairs in the kitchen. I could smell bacon, too, over the kebab stink, which she'd probably cooked hours before. She must have found it obscene how late I stayed in bed after those sessions, a woman so permanently on the go like her, who rose at six come Hell or high water, but she never did say anything to me about it.

The most she ever said was,

"Late night, last night, was it?" with really just the slightest hint of a judgey inflection, to which I would tiredly nod, rub my face clownishly and just say,

"Ha. Yeah," like all the idiot politicians do these days because they think it makes them look relatable.

As if she was acting out of a sixth sense for servitude, I heard my Nan climbing the stairs just as I propped myself upright in my blanket swaddled crib and tried to smile. I was so relieved the bed wasn't pissed, I can't tell you. I'd done it once before at her place and the embarrassment had nearly killed me. The silent way she'd helped me clean up afterward, taking the soaked sheets in a soggy bundle without looking in my eyes. Quietly laying down new blankets, new linen, of which she seemed to have an endless supply. Fucking awful. I mean really, powerfully pathetic.

She pushed open the door and placed a strong tea with two sugars on the bedside table next to me. She always put in one more sugar than I was used to, but I secretly liked it, like a little bonus treat for which I was entirely blameless, so I never really took it up with her. Without even looking at me and without any great emphasis or interest she said, as she turned to leave,

"You might want to get up, love, there's something on the news about America. Some planes missing or something…"

Planes, plural? Missing? My interest was piqued. My Nan's own interest in and appreciation of current affairs had, at one point in her life, been fairly keen. The whole family was proud of their prowess in Trivial Pursuit, the still popular board game which served as a sort of litmus test for intelligence in our clan, and Nan could always hold her own, but she had lost some of that spark in those latter years, so the fact that she would even mention anything to me had to mean it was significant. I leant forward and groped at the bottom of my bed for the crumpled denim of my kicked-off jeans and pulled my cheap mobile phone out of a distressingly crusty pocket. I checked my messages.

There were a number from fellas off my politics course and most of them just said something like *Fuck!* or *Fucking hell*, so I knew something must have really been up.

It was 2:30pm. I know. A disgrace. I grabbed my tea, perched it precariously on the toilet window ledge whilst I relieved myself, then stalked downstairs in a T-shirt, undies and socks, carrying a thick blanket like some out-of-era Dickens' character. I went straight to the front room and cranked on the gas fire. I was lucky that it was a workday, a Tuesday as it happens, so my uncle, who lived with Nan, was out of the house. I had the room to myself. I plonked myself in 'little' grandad's old armchair, right in front of the telly. He'd been dead twelve years or more but it was still somehow *his* chair. I wrapped myself up in the blanket and banged on the BBC news.

The scenes were chaos. Even out of the mouths of the usually sober BBC reporters, there was a palpable sense of events beyond their comprehension. I'd come to the news before the second plane had hit, so there was still this sense that maybe, I mean, just maybe it was all some kind of terrible accident. Reports were coming in faster than they could field about planes that were missing, changing flight paths, US fighter forces scrambled in the skies. I was gripped. I hardly noticed my Nan enter the room and place a stack of toasted bacon butties on the arm of my chair as I simply stared, slack jawed, at the utterly mental madness unfolding in real time on the screen before me.

Without taking my eyes off the screen, I reached to my side and picked up a sandwich slathered with brown sauce. She had made them the way she knew I liked, on lightly toasted white bread, because my pa had eaten them the same way when he'd lodged with her between shifts. He was a Firefighter in the local station once upon a time and would often stay overnight when he was on days or between shifts. I stuffed half the butty into my mouth. I slurped back the deliciously sweet tea. My mind was running with a hundred questions like every other fuck on the planet glued to their TV set at that moment, but all of those thoughts could be distilled into one simple sentence at a push, which was: This is very, very bad.

And that is when the second plane hit. I had, in the most macabre and voyeuristic sense possible, arrived just in time. The news anchors – because now I was skipping between channels – interrupted their halfway reserved commentaries with suddenly excited, almost panicked, segues:

"And we're just hearing…" and even,

"Oh gosh."

And then came the pictures. In my memory, the video clip that was used only emphasised the horror. Slightly grainy footage taken apparently from a handheld recorder or a mobile phone showed the second – or was it the third – plane? I forget what had happened with The Pentagon at this point. Anyway, a plane was slamming into the second tower of the World Trade Center. It entered one side whole and emerged from the other transformed: just an awful belching lick of molten steel and flame. The audio on the video was a woman gasping.

"Ohhh god," she says, over and over, and forever now, because the clip is played back endlessly in the coming hours, days, months, years. That gasp, that shock, that "Oh god," became a part of our collective memory, a part of us, those that witnessed it. But not for my Nan. She was in the other room.

For a moment I was stunned. I dropped the sandwich in my lap and simply stared. Then, another of those thoughts most likely shared with a billion or more minds in that exact moment formed itself into one single, elongated word. This time: Fuuuuuuuuuuck. Because we knew. We knew then, in that moment, that this thing was *meant*. Any doubt was vaporised with the lives of the people in that aeroplane or on the floors of that iconic building. Those American lives. That American icon. And anyone with a speck of sense for global politics knew in that instant what had to come next. Somebody was going to have to pay. Some people, in some part of the world, would have to pay for those American lives and pay in blood. I had to talk to someone.

I shouted out, "Nan. Nan! Come 'ere. You've got to see this," but got no reply.

I shouted out again, still gawping, and waited, but she didn't come through. She was probably reading yesterday's *Echo* or something, like she often did, or smoking a ciggie, but she was clearly determined to just leave me to it in the front room with the TV and whatever was 'Going on over there', as she often said. But I couldn't have that. I had to talk to someone. This thing was so huge and had so many awful ramifications. I just had to get up and share it, share my thoughts, with someone. I got out of my seat and strode towards the back of the house, still half-dressed. She was, as I'd guessed, sitting in the back kitchen, as we always called it, as though there was some other kitchen in some other location, which there very definitely was not. She was sitting there smoking a ciggie, staring into the middle distance.

There is a particular smell of cigarette smoke, old toast and cooking oil over chilled air that still transports me right into that kitchen. I can walk into a room, usually canteens or staff kitchens in municipal kinds of spaces, and that combination of smells hits and takes me back to that room and – more often than not – that moment. My Nan sitting there, smoking, a tired and melancholy look on her face.

My Nan had the kind of face that always looked thoughtful, whatever was going on in her head. She had a long, straight nose – that I gladly inherited – and deep lines and creases all over of the kind that Native American chiefs or squaws have as they age, attesting to a conglomeration of wisdom or hardship, which is probably more or less the same thing. She had deep set hazel eyes with beautiful dark lashes – which I did not get – though my father has them and my brother too, and a strong jaw line which could not be disguised despite the sagging of her aging flesh. It was a noble face. If she simply sat still and closed, or half closed her eyes, her face looked regal and melancholy and wise, all at the same time. It is how I see her when I try to bring her to mind, looking like she did then, in the back kitchen. But I didn't ask her what was wrong, because that was just her face and I had far too much to say.

"Nan, you are not going to believe this…" I started up, then I explained it all to her.

I explained what had happened. I explained the shock, the impact, the dreadful burst of flame, the gasps of the reporters and the fact that there were still more planes in the air. I explained what it meant for international global relations, who the likely suspects were, how this was bound to trigger an aggressive foreign policy response and recast intercultural relations between the West and the Arab world for decades, possibly forever. I explained to her, a 70-odd-year-old woman from the Dingle, Liverpool, why she really should be interested in this because it involved us all, everyone in the world, and the ramifications would touch everyone's lives in some big or small way, for certain. But she was not convinced. She still, if anything, looked a little distant.

"I don't know, love," she said, quietly, "It just seems very sad, to me."

I laughed.

"Yeah, you can say that again," I said, and shook my head in disbelief thinking it was really very simple, what she'd just said. I laughed and loved her for it and didn't ask her what was wrong, because that wasn't on my mind. It wasn't on my mind what could be distracting her, a woman of more than seven decades of experiences, from one of the biggest events in recent history. That rankles now. It could have been all kinds of things, of course, because she carried the worries of our whole family at different points, truth be told. If someone had financial problems, she'd help them out. If someone was going through a break-up or drinking too much (ha!) or spinning out in general, she'd hear about it. She was always chief counsel, whether she wanted the role or not. And her own health was suffering too, round that period. It was around that time she went in for a heart operation and was never really the same after it. She became forgetful and confused. So that might also have been bothering her – she might have seen it coming. I'll never know, will I? Because I didn't ask.

Instead, I went back into the front room, cosy now with the gas fire blaring, though Nan usually kept it low to save on the bills and devoured the rest of the sandwiches along with every last bit of footage that kept pouring out of that TV screen. I was glued to it. I watched both towers fall, live. Imagine that: live footage of such an event. Anyone too young or too old just has no idea. It got dark and as the hours passed my Nan came in and out, bringing biscuits and more butties and all kinds of stuff. I told her I didn't want a proper tea – that I'd get something from the chippy later – and she seemed fine with that. Sometimes she sat down for a bit to look at the pictures with me and ask a question here or there, but God knows what we talked about because I was, by that point, mesmerised, off on my own little trip.

I didn't try to talk to her about it anymore. I didn't spend that night talking to her about it, or about anything else, for that matter, like I should have done. I can't say why, exactly. I regret it now. Maybe, on some level, I thought I was too clever for her, though the thought shames me. Perhaps I felt it wasn't what she wanted, after the sad way she'd responded at first. I don't know. I could have tried to get her thoughts, for all the awkwardness I thought I'd feel – or imagined that she might – but I didn't. My uncle E came back a bit later and I had it out with him for a while, over a beer, then I went to the offy and bought some cans to really take the edge off the hangover once and for all. I sat upstairs in the spare room, head fucking blown, beer cans on the floor and blankets around my knees, drinking and writing down my very important thoughts in case the world needed to hear them later. Which, it turns out, was unnecessary.

I texted a few mates, "What the fuck?" and "When you getting back?" I went back to my uni digs, buzzing with it all, just a few days later. I can't even remember how I left it with Nan; probably just a quick goodbye, love you, see you in a few weeks. I know I just assumed she'd always be there, like she always had been, for this start of the school year ritual thing I had going.

Back in uni, it was different. I got to talk it all through there, plenty, going over and over it with smart arses like myself, on the seemingly endless piss. We had so many opinions. What this meant for the global geo-political landscape. The impact of mainland attack on the American psyche. We loved it. We drank and drank, and we talked and talked. We talked a whole lot of shit those next few years and we drank plenty too. It was a hoot.

Mary Smillie died of complications resultant from a stroke on the 4th of June, 2004. She was seventy-nine.

Acknowledgements

Whilst it is fairly common for acknowledgements to start with the line "this book couldn´t have happened without so and so", I´d like to think on this particular occasion, it will be seen for the statement of fact it really is. I could not have published this book, in this way, without the direct support, both moral and financial, of the following people:

Brigid Atterton, Marina Barthe Astiarrage, Rüdiger and Susanna Biedemann, Natalie and Sebastien Bölefahr, Natasha Butler, Inge and Peter Corkill, Phil Corkill, Jodie Dickinson, Barbara Ding, Markus Elner, Fiona Goff, Alex Gavaghan, Dulcie and Nathan Goss, Heinz Groß, Sarah Higgins, Jo Kane, Vicky Kieth, Jo Kim, Margarot Kontosorou, Jack Mullett, Anna Meckelnborg, Dominique Nothnagel, Nicola Owen, Andrew and Helen Parsons, Sarah Roberts, Peter Standige, Angelika and Hans-Jürgen Schöpf, Daffydd Singleton, Andrew and Joanna Smillie, Jenny Smillie, Wendy and Gary W. Smillie, Alice and Darren Tomlinson, Johanna Wadle, Dan Wilson, Julia Windhorst, Thomas Wright and Lois Young.

Thank you, all of you, for your contributions and I hope the final product has given you some cause to fondly appraise that decision, or, at the very least, not to entirely regret it.

I obviously want to make special mention of my ma and pa, Wendy and Gary Smillie, to whom the book is dedicated. They have been my chief inspirers and supporters (as well as nourishers, teachers, coaches, all-round exceptionally good eggers) through all the years of my existence, so this is very much for them.

My little brother, Andy, and older sister, Jenny, have also been an incredible lifelong support, so this book is a little bit for them too.

Special thanks should also go to my partner, Dominique, for all her love and support and, of course, for the idea behind this crowdfunding venture. Thanks, doll. Thanks too to my previous partners for indulging my favourite hobby, and in some special cases, championing whatever "talent" I might possess. It was and is appreciated.

Big, big thanks to my good friend Markus Elner for the excellent cover design, done purely out of the love of his heart, that brought a simple idea of mine to life. Check out his stuff at https://linktr.ee/Mad_moerges or on Instagram @Mad_moerges.

Massive thanks are also due to Adam Paxman, who sprang to my aid at the last minute, despite a raging cold and a busy schedule, to provide an incredibly thorough proof-reading that improved the final copy immeasurably. You should all immediately go and purchase and read his excellent back-catalogue– most of which is available on Amazon.

For further editing and appraisal, there are a number of unpaid volunteers that I really should thank. Paul M Clark, for his words of wisdom and encouragement. Peter Corkill for his fastidious editing and important tips. Dave Small, Jodie Dickinson, Chris Anderson, Hannah Charnock, Phil Corkill, Anna Meckelnborg, Desiree Nothnagel, Luke Goss, Andy Frisby and a number of others whose names temporarily (in this moment) and now permanently (in print) escape me. All these fine folks have read and critiqued my stories at different points and I truly appreciate their contribution.

Further than that aforementioned group of ne´er-do-wells, there are a host of friends, family and wider influences that I must thank for giving me the pushes, prods and praise that I have needed to persevere. Amongst them I should mention: Ms. Hayes and Mrs. Lewis Jones, my high school English teachers, the latter of whom introduced me to Raymond Carver – the master of this particular form of writing. Also important to mention are Mary Smillie – my nan, whose storytelling legacy lives on, Carl Atterton, Sally Lewis, Fran Atterton, Dave "The Hat" McGowan, Orlando Harrison, Mark Percy, the music of the Cubical more generally, Paul Wilson, Ryan Gosling (why not?), Dagmar Tenssae, Michael Hopwood and many other fantastic humans who have touched my life.

In terms of resources and websites, etc., my thanks to Lang Leav, whose work I quote in the story *To Lie With Dogs*, Wikipedia (a lot), www.wolf.org, www.rewildingeurope.com, the reading room at Manchester Central Library, the TV series *Celebrity Big Brother*, the stories of Raymond Carver, the meadows of Wales and the ale-houses of countless towns and cities.

Thanks, of course, to Matador for the publishing expertise to make this a final product I can be proud of.

Finally, thanks to my daughter Anouk, my real-life human offspring, for being so incredibly cute and for giving me the kick up the you-know-what needed to get this word-based baby into the world.

Thanks all. You´re so very bloody lovely.

Lightning Source UK Ltd.
Milton Keynes UK
UKHW021954260722
406415UK00005B/211